Jack was looking for something else today—a pretty face, a soft voice, a sassy smile.

Mike's daughter was the complete package. To hear Mike tell it, his daughter was a fair ranch hand herself, not to mention good student, good teacher, good cook, good mother, good-looking—hell, you could zone out, tune back in and Mike was *still* talking about Lily.

She'd given him her name, caught his eye, and he'd been damn grateful for the shelter of his hat brim. Felt like he'd touched a live electrical wire. Crazy. First time he'd felt that kind of sensation absent a power source. Unless that's what she was.

Damn, what was he, sixteen?

Dear Reader,

The hero of my first Harlequin Special Edition was a rodeo cowboy. I've since put dozens of cowboys between the covers of Special Edition—bull riders, ropers, horse trainers, ranchers and cowboys for hire. Jack McKenzie is what's known as a "day worker." He's a highly skilled ranch hand who hires out to as many ranchers as he can fit into his schedule.

Times have changed since my husband and I were in the cattle ranching business, and few operations can afford the full-time "hired man." The small-scale cattleman faces seemingly overwhelming competition from mega ranches. It's a classic David and Goliath story, and the day worker is one of David's best allies.

With no shortage of work for an experienced cowboy during calving season, Jack is hard-pressed to devote his time to one aging Montana rancher who's too stubborn to admit that his health might be failing. But Jack knows what it's like to be a loner. His sympathy for his boss is only the beginning of this cowboy's commitment when Mike's daughter, Lily, reluctantly returns home.

I love writing about cowboys, and I know you love reading about them. I hope you'll check in with me on Facebook, my website kathleeneagle.com, and my blog, ridingwiththetopdown.wordpress.com. We'll talk cowboys and Indians, horses and kids and books, books, books.

Happy tales!

Kathleen Eagle

KATHLEEN EAGLE

ONE LESS LONELY COWBOY

HARLEQUIN®SPECIAL EDITION®

Recycling programs
for this product may
not exist in your area.

ISBN-13: 978-0-373-65727-8

ONE LESS LONELY COWBOY

Copyright © 2013 by Kathleen Eagle

Printed in U.S.A.

KATHLEEN EAGLE

published her first book, a Romance Writers of America Golden Heart Award winner, with Silhouette Books in 1984. Since then, she has published more than forty books, including historical and contemporary, series and single title, earning her nearly every award in the industry. Her books have consistently appeared on regional and national bestseller lists, including the *USA TODAY* list and the *New York Times* extended bestseller list.

Kathleen lives in Minnesota with her husband, who is Lakota Sioux. They have three grown children and three lively grandchildren.

For David and Shawna
May you live happily ever after

Chapter One

Iris reminded her mother of a hatchling popping out of its shell. She'd slept through much of western North Dakota, missed crossing the state line, and now she was about to get her first look at her new stomping grounds. Her new airspace. Plenty of air, plenty of space—two more points Lily Reardon could add to the plus side of the next pointless discussion about the move they had to make. It didn't matter that Iris only bothered with one minus—leaving her friends—against Lily's multitude of pluses, or that the discussion was no longer a discussion but a fait accompli. It would come up again, mainly because Iris was waking up in more ways than one.

She blinked, head bobbing atop a long, slightly wobbly neck as she emerged from the white folds of her old Minky blanket, still the hatchling for another second, maybe two. Blink, blink. No judgment in the big blue eyes that searched first for assurance that Mommy was nearby. Last year's Iris. Lily's little girl.

Then the curtain came down in those eyes.

"Where are we?"

It wasn't the question that was hard to take; it was the tone. It was like the landscape surrounding the second-hand Chevy that was one missed payment away from getting repossessed: beautifully straightforward and unforgiving. The answer wasn't important.

"We're almost there."

Iris drew a deep breath as she took a look at either side of the two-lane road. Winter had receded from the brown grasslands, but spring wasn't ready to put up any green shoots. Nights were still too cold, and the sky was still untrustworthy. The beauty would come. They only had to wait a little longer, drive a little farther. But Iris could only know what she was seeing here and now. Montana was Lily's birthplace. It had narrowly missed being Iris's.

"I hope there's a 'there' there," Iris said. "I don't see any here."

Lily chuckled. Whether trying her patience or plumbing her trove of trivia, her daughter loved testing her. Being both mother and teacher, Lily lived in double jeopardy.

Lily took the bait. "You know where that comes from, don't you? 'There's no there there'?"

"Gertrude Stein."

Lily smiled at the road ahead. Point for knowing the answer, extra point for not saying *duh*. They passed a turn marked by the sign that told Lily they were getting close. Iris had stopped noticing signs the day before, two or three hundred miles back. She'd been asleep when Lily had turned off the road at a truck stop near Dickinson, North Dakota, when she'd started nodding off herself.

"She was talking about California," Iris said. "Can you imagine?"

"Oakland."

"What*ever.*"

Point docked on Lily's mental scoreboard. But this wasn't the time for a tally.

"Cali-freakin'-*fornia,*" Iris said, as though she knew the place firsthand. "If there's no 'there' *there,* I quit."

"Quit what?"

"The journey. Life's a journey, right? Literally

and figuratively both. And this—" Iris made a sweeping gesture toward the brown fields and foothills beyond the windshield. "—is just a lay-over. Who goes to a place like…" She sucked in the deep breath her dramatic sigh required. "Back to my original question. Where are we?"

"As far west as your thirteen-year journey has taken you so far. We just passed Lowdown, Mon-tana."

"Who goes to Lowdown, Montana, Mom? *Who?* Oh, God, we do." Iris slid back down, tuck-ing her chin into her blanket. "We two, we un-happy two, and we don't even stop in Lowdown. We drive right through on our way to Bottom Feeder Farm."

"The Rocking R Ranch."

Iris groaned. "That is so Roy Rogers, Mom."

Lily laughed. "And what do you know about Roy Rogers?"

"Enough to beat Rachel Varney at TV trivia. We were running neck and neck until we hit the fifties, and then I—" She slid one palm across the other and whistled through her teeth. "Because I never miss *American Pickers* on TV."

"You and your grandfather will get along just fine. He never throws anything away." *Except peo-ple,* Lily reminded herself. But her quick follow-up reminder—*water under the bridge*—helped her keep her foot on the gas pedal. Her father would be glad to have them. His words. No qualifiers, no pregnant pauses.

"OMG, speaking of Roy Rogers…" Iris straightened in her seat. Lily chuckled. Iris hadn't noticed old man Tyree's fence post boots until they'd passed the first few. Old boots capped steel fence posts along the right of way for at least a mile, kicking their weathered heels at heaven. Iris swung her head back and forth, counting under her breath as they passed each one. Finally she laughed. "Is this what passes for recycling here?"

"I never thought of it that way." Some of the leather looked like beef jerky. Lily wondered whether her father's neighbor was kicking up his heels somewhere beyond the big sky. "The exhibit has been growing ever since I can remember. Supposedly the man who lived here started it when he got stuck up to his boot tops during a gully washer and he hung them up there thinking the rain would clean them off."

"Did it?"

"I don't even know whether the story's true." Lily glanced over at her daughter, hiking her eyebrows. "Could be a rural legend. Think Snopes dot com would have something to say about that?"

"I think it's called 'Lies My Mother Told Me.'"

"Oh, come on. Lighten up."

"You kids with your boots on the ground," Iris mocked in a crackly voice. "We had to leave ours on the fence post so we didn't lose them in the mud. We walked to school." She wagged her forefinger at the windshield. "Twenty miles each way. Barefoot."

"Only when it rained," Lily said with a smile.

"Carrying your Roy Rogers lunch boxes, which are now worth more than— Don't tell me this is it," Iris said, as Lily flicked the turn signal. The last fence post boot was a speck in the rearview mirror. A break in the four-wire fence was marked by a sparsely graveled approach, a new cattle guard and an old sign. "Mom, there's nothing here. Just... Omigod, you weren't kidding. The Rocking R Ranch. Really."

"Really."

It was hard to keep a straight face, but Lily had to put forth the effort. Otherwise she wasn't sure whether her mouth would turn up or down. She hadn't seen much of her father since she'd left the ranch over thirteen years ago. She'd seen him twice, to be exact, and both times he'd been the one to initiate the contact, and pay his only child and grandchild a visit in Minneapolis. It had been four years since the last visit. She'd told herself she was going to make this trip with Iris one of these days, just as soon as the right day came along. It never had.

Lily wasn't kidding herself thinking this was the elusive *right* day. On the right day she would have been at the top of her game, returning on terms of her choosing. If she'd made the time when times were good, this trip might not be so difficult. But she hadn't. Once she'd lost her job, times had gone from tight to tough to agonizingly tense, but she wouldn't call for help from her father until she had no other choice. And no home plus no money equaled no other choice.

So here they were, and here, at the very least, was a place to be. The house hadn't changed—a box with a top—but it promised a roof over their heads, over doors that opened and closed, over quiet rooms with safe beds. It wasn't home anymore, not since she had walked away carrying Iris inside her. But it was a place to be. Nothing quite like an eviction notice to put a necessity once taken for granted into perspective. All they had now was each other, and Iris would never have less. She would never be alone, certainly not by Lily's choice. Pride didn't go down easily, but it did go quietly. For Iris's sake.

"Does the Rocking R Ranch have wi-fi?" Iris's voice had lost all its edge, all its humor. Could this be the sound of a thirteen-year-old's reality setting in?

"I don't know." It wasn't a lie. She didn't know for sure, and what were the words *I doubt it* really worth?

"It didn't occur to me to ask," Iris said. "Until now. Not that it would have mattered."

Lily stared straight ahead. They were nearing the place she'd last seen in the rearview mirror of a friend's pickup. Not a boyfriend's pickup. The driver hadn't been the father of her unborn child. Molly Taylor had driven her to Glendive, where she'd boarded a Greyhound bus and headed for Minneapolis, which hadn't been exactly what Mom had it cracked up to be. Nothing ever was. But it was a place to be until Lily took matters into her own hands and made it more than that. She'd worked her butt off to get her degree and her own place and her teaching position, and she'd almost gotten tenure. Almost. But then she'd lost her job, and she hadn't been optimistic about the prospect of getting on at another school. *You pay your dues so you don't have to take any more chances.* She'd had her standards, her requirements—damn it, she'd earned the right to hold out for more. At the very least for nothing less. Security, maybe?

Okay, subsistence.

How about survival?

She had fought it, cursed it, and finally she'd made her peace with reality. But she wasn't ready to force the whole reality enchilada on a thirteen-year-old. There had to be some scrap of fantasy left for Iris. Lily couldn't provide internet, but surely she could come up with something wonderful and wireless.

She pulled the car around back of the house, and there was her something.

"Horses, Iris." The old barn's new metal roof glinted in the sun. Two sorrels stood in the small pasture outside the corral, where a man was working a beautiful black-and-white paint on a lunge line. "You've always wanted to ride," Lily said. "Now's your chance."

"Oh." Iris released the buckle on her seat belt as she leaned closer to the windshield. "Hey. That's not Grandpa." Closer still. Lily wondered whether it was time for an eye exam. "Mom, who's the cowboy?"

"No idea."

"Really? Good."

Iris got out of the car, shut the door a little harder than necessary and met her mother on the other side. Lily was pretty sure she'd made the entire move without taking her eyes off the corral, not even for the motley-colored dog that darted out from behind the barn growling and then, at a glance from the cowboy, quickly retreated to the fence and sat. Lily glanced back at the cowboy, whose connection with the dog was clearly below the radar.

"Okay, this place is suddenly looking a lot better." The comment was sotto voce, not that the cowboy seemed to be paying them any mind. "His pants are kinda tight and geeky, but maybe that's not such a bad thing."

"They *fit*." Lily gave her daughter a *who-are-you?* look. "Not that it matters."

Iris squinted, gave a tight smile. "I saw him first."

"Iris, really."

"You keep telling me to look on the bright side. I finally found one." She turned back to the corral. The man was concentrating on his horse. "We should go introduce ourselves."

"We should go present ourselves to your grandfather. He knows we're coming, but…" Lily put her arm around her daughter's shoulders and urged herself by urging Iris toward the back door of the house. "I wasn't sure exactly when."

After several knocks the door still stood closed.

"Is it locked?" Iris wanted to know.

"We'll wait for him to let us in." Lily could feel the doubt, the disbelief, the adolescent impatience growing on her left flank. Or was it really her own uncertain center, the feel of her tail stuck between her legs? Her head was telling her to get on with it—the first few moments would be the hardest—but the strings to her limbs were tied somehow to the knot in her stomach. She glanced at Iris, who questioned her with a puckered brow.

"You can try it if you want." With a gesture toward the doorknob, Lily took a step back.

Seriously? the voice in her head scolded.

"He's *your* father." Iris's frown deepened. "He's expecting us, isn't he?"

"Yes, but…I should have called him before we left. Or when we stopped in Fargo, maybe." Lily gave her head a quick shake. She was making a complete fool of herself. "I don't know what I was thinking. Trying to time it just right, I guess. After chores, before bed. You don't want to…"…*get him on the phone when he's been drinking.* She turned away from the door and looked elsewhere. "Let's ask the cowboy."

"Oh, let's."

Iris's delight was understandable. From a distance the man was promising. He knew what he was doing, and he looked good doing it. Smooth, sure, confident. The horse didn't question it, and neither did the dog. Lily wanted some of that right now. The confidence, not the man. But the closer they got, the better he looked. His long, lean body, his deft hands, his handsome face all kept faith with the promise he'd shown at a distance. Lily was sure he'd noticed them, but the easy-loping paint had his full attention.

A man who minded his business. Always impressive.

Iris was the first to call out to him. A bold

"Hi!" No shrinking violet, her daughter, but Lily sensed a little deflation when the cowboy spared no more than a glance and a nod. She laid her hand on Iris's shoulder and pressed on. The ball was in Mom's court now.

"We're looking for Mike Reardon," Lily called out as she stepped up on the bottom corral rail and folded her forearms over the top one.

A low-pitched, authoritative "Ho" changed the horse's pace. The lunge line went slack, and the cowboy finally turned about half his attention to the women. "You came to the right place at the wrong time. He went into town."

"I'm Lily, Mike's daughter. He went to Lowdown?"

"I'm Iris, the granddaughter." She'd scrambled up two corral rails, putting her head and shoulders above her mother.

"Jack McKenzie." He touched a gloved finger to the brim of his black hat. "The hired hand."

"Really. Grandpa has a hired hand." Iris glanced down, grinning at her mother.

What a difference a cowboy made, Lily thought.

"That sounds so cool. Like a real ranch," Iris added.

"Like Roy Rogers?" Lily teased.

"The Double R Bar. I know my TV trivia." Iris wasn't going to let the man go too easily. "What are you hired to do, exactly? Are you like a real cowboy?"

"Iris…"

The cowboy cracked a smile, which changed the whole attitude of his chiseled face, put a spark in his dark eyes and gave his full lips potentially delicious animation. He let the rope slide loosely through his grip as he turned his back to the horse and approached the fence. The line went slack as the horse followed, seemingly of its own volition. "As real as they come these days. I'm all about chasing cows." He pulled off his right glove and offered Lily a handshake. "Mike talks about you a lot. Does he know you're coming?"

"I just talked to him a couple of days ago. Yes, he said we should…" She watched him offer Iris the same greeting, and it occurred to her for the first time that the man was American Indian, at least in part. It was the handshake—a brief, warm, easy touch offered to everyone present, adult and child alike.

She glanced up, suddenly anxious. "Is he okay?"

"He's doing good, yeah. He doesn't—"

"I know. He says he goes to meetings and all that. Just making sure we aren't walking into…" Lily clamped down on her tongue. Too much information. The drinking was something she would deal with like an adult. She'd been to a few meetings herself. Adult children of people who shouldn't have been parents. The group had another name, but that was what it came down to. She gave half a shrug and offered a tight smile. "Making sure nothing's changed since, you know, he invited us here."

The cowboy answered her shrug in kind. "I just work here."

"Of course. I'm sorry. I should have—"

"That's a great-looking horse," Iris put in cheerfully. "Is he Grandpa's?"

Jack grinned. "She's mine. Mike lets me keep my horses here. The filly's just getting settled in. Got her out of that wild-horse adoption program down in South Dakota."

"She's wild? She doesn't look wild."

He laughed. "You can't tell by looking. Kinda like people."

"So you can't ride her?"

"Not yet."

"What's her name?"

He turned his smile to his horse, tipped his head as though he expected the answer to come from her. "Yeah, we haven't quite decided."

"I'm named for a flower," Iris said. "So's Mom."

"Was that his idea?" Jack nodded toward the house. Iris and Lily turned their heads, following the direction of his gesture and becoming aware of the soundless arrival of the man they'd been looking for. "Hell of a romantic, that guy. Nice flower garden you've got here, Mike."

Parking rules must have changed, Lily thought. *Don't want no vehicle left in the front of the house. The less of our business people can see, the better.*

Her father's appearance registered hard on the heels of that thought. Maybe he walked more quietly than she remembered because he'd lost some weight. But he'd gained a ready smile, and Iris went straight to him.

"A bright spot for sure." His voice had gone the way of his walk—quieter, a little raspy. But any vigor the years had taken away, the blue eyes that greeted Lily's made up for with a vibrancy she hadn't seen before. "Real nice surprise, too," he said as he accepted Iris's eager hug in the way of a man who was trying something out that he'd spent much of his life avoiding.

"Surprise?" Lily wasn't going to compound the awkwardness with more hugging.

"You didn't say for sure. I mean..." He gave Iris's back a parting pat. "I'm glad you're here. Look at this one, will you? You were just..." His leathery hand measured four feet up from the ground. "Maybe less. Growing like a weed."

"A flower," Jack said, turning to Iris. "What kind did you say?"

"Iris."

"Iris and Lily." He touched a finger to the brim of his hat. "Pleasure."

"Pleasure?" Iris whispered.

"To meet us," Lily explained, as they watched the cowboy amble across the corral, the paint homing in on his shoulder and following along like a well-trained dog. She glanced at Iris. She knew cowboys. *Had known.* One cowboy, anyway. It could be mesmerizing, just watching them walk with fluid, natural ease. "They don't like to waste words."

"*They?* Who's *they,* Mom. Don't tell me you're being—"

"Men." Lily chuckled. "*Some* men. Westerners. Right, Dad?"

"We don't like to waste anything. We're conservative. Or conservationists." He gave Lily an oddly hopeful look. "Which is it, English teacher?"

"I'd say you're both." She wasn't sure what he was hoping for. The opening for a touchy-feely moment between them had come and gone. "I guess I should've called again, but I thought you knew we were on our way after you gave us a green light."

"I was gonna fix up the bedrooms. Yours hasn't changed since you left." Mike laid his stiff hand on his granddaughter's shoulder. "You want your mama's old room, girl? It's small, but it's—"

"*Iris,* Dad. *I'm* 'girl.' She's Iris." Lily tried to exchange a glance with her daughter, but Iris wasn't doing her part. The cowboy and his horse were more interesting.

Yeah, okay, so maybe they were. But even so, Lily wasn't letting anyone call Iris *girl.*

"Haven't had a girl on the place since you left, and now there's two. Gonna take some getting used to."

"We'll make it easy on you, Dad. I haven't forgotten how to drive a tractor."

"*You* can drive a tractor?" Doubting Iris was back.

"She can, but she won't have to," her father said. "Drivin' tractor's about all I do lately. Jack takes care of the heavy lifting. If you can still bake that strawberry rhubarb pie you used to make, that's all I ask." He winked at his granddaughter. "What's your specialty, g—Iris?"

Iris laughed. "Guy-ris? How's that, Mom?" She raked her finger through her strawberry-blond bob. "I'm letting my hair grow out. Does Jack live here?"

"I wish he did." Mike glanced at the weathered red barn, where the cowboy and his filly had taken refuge. The dog was gone, too. "Jack's a day worker, and he's in high demand. I can't afford him full-time."

"What's a day worker?" Iris wanted to know.

"Cowboy for hire. Jack's a top hand. I let him keep his horses here, and like I said, he takes care of the heavy stuff. That's where he lives." Mike pointed to a long white gooseneck trailer, hooked up to a red dually pickup that was parked upwind of the barn.

"Isn't that for horses?"

"Part of it is." Mike folded his arms across his narrow chest. "He's a gypsy, Jack is. That's his wagon."

Iris smiled, casting a wistful glance toward the open barn door. "So that's what Gypsies look like."

"Jack's part Chippewa, Cree, something like that. Métis, he calls himself. Mixed-blood. Gotta admit, I never paid much attention to the different tribes around here until Jack came along."

"I had Native American friends in Minnesota," Iris said. "That's not the same as Gypsy."

"All I know for sure is Jack McKenzie is one hell of a cowboy. Without him, I don't know… I'd'a been in deep trouble this winter."

"Is he married or anything?" Iris persisted.

"He ain't married. Don't know about *anything*. He's got a couple kids up around Wolf Point. Goes up there to visit pretty regular." Mike's eyes narrowed in amusement. "You writin' a book or somethin'?"

"He's a hottie." Iris gave her grandfather her recently perfected bug eyes. "Duh."

"That's it, Iris. No *duh,*" Lily said.

"Sorry, Grandpa." Iris hung her head. Like the blush that followed, the hangdog posture was rare. "It just means, like, *obviously,*" she explained quietly.

"Hottie, huh?" Mike chuckled. "Like I said, it's gonna take some getting used to, havin' girls around."

Mike helped them carry luggage and a few boxes through the kitchen, down the hall and into the bedrooms. Lily said more was being shipped—she hadn't been able to fit everything in the car—but what she didn't say was that she'd sold everything she could. She wasn't looking forward to the day when the boxes arrived and Iris started missing things. Among other things, her bike had been sold, and all but three of her stuffed animals had gone to the Salvation Army.

Iris had left the apartment each time Lily asked for help sorting their stuff out. She'd been warned. *If you leave it to me, you might be sorry later.* Lily had been grateful for Iris's silence on the matter, but she knew her daughter's denial had been considerably deeper than her own. Sooner or later there would be tears.

It felt strange to haul her suitcase full of women's clothes to their temporary quarters in the bedroom

she'd painted pink and green when she was a teenager. Stranger still, the room hadn't changed. Her
father hadn't been kidding about that. As much as
he'd hated her music, he hadn't taken her posters
down. The Dave Matthews Band, Hootie and the
Blowfish, beautiful Gloria Estefan, whose dress
was the same shade of pink she'd chosen for her
walls. The quilt her grandmother had made—the
one she regretted not taking with her—the Breyer
horses, the ruffled café curtains, everything looked
the same as the day she'd hauled her pregnant self
out to Molly's pickup.

"Wow, Mom, this was you?"

Lily turned to find her daughter standing next
to the chest of drawers and holding a silver picture frame. There were more frames on top of
the chest. They hadn't been there before, so she
had to step up and take a look. With a nod she acknowledged her high school portrait, even though
it was hard for her to recognize the carefree smile
on the girl in the picture. Not the way she remembered the time the picture was taken. What
had she been doing that day to put that look in
her eyes?

"Wow. You were hot."

Lily laughed. "Duh."

"Nope. No duh." Iris set the picture back on the
bureau and picked up another one. Lily standing
beside Juniper. "Whose horse is this?"

"Mine. Well…" Could she really say that? She'd left the horse, along with everything else in the room. "She was mine then."

"Beautiful." Iris set the picture back in its place and turned her attention to the rest of the array. "It's almost worth it, coming here, just to see what you looked like when you were young."

"When I was young?" Aloud Lily chuckled, but in her mind she puzzled over the mere fact that the pictures were on display, neatly framed.

"Okay, young-*ger*. How old were you here?" Iris pointed to a picture of Lily wearing a dress. A rare image for those days.

"About fifteen."

"I hope I look this good when I'm…" Iris rested her hand on top of a small album. Lily recognized the flowered cover. "Are there any of my father?"

"I don't know what's still here, sweetie." She knew she'd bought that album herself, but she couldn't remember what she'd put in it.

Iris tapped her fingers on the cover. "You're gonna let me find out for myself?"

"It's your room. I didn't take much with me when I moved out, so it'll be fun to see what you dig up."

Fun? Maybe that was pushing it. But oddly enough, the word wasn't hard to say. It could be fun. The girl in the pictures looked surprisingly happy.

Iris turned to one of two sets of wall shelves her father had put up—grudgingly, as Lily remembered—for her books and other treasures. He'd complained about putting holes in the wall. "What's all this about?" Iris asked.

"I was in 4-H. State fair competitions, mostly. Different kinds of..." Iris picked up a small silver horse. A big blue ribbon was looped around the base. "That's for Western Pleasure."

"'Grand champion,'" Iris read aloud from the ribbon. She examined more ribbons, all dusty, mostly faded, but the recognition stamped in gold still shown. "First place. Second place. First place." Grinning broadly, she looked up at her mother. "You got first place in rabbits?"

Lily couldn't help smiling. "I raised rabbits one summer. Hoppsie and Poppsie."

"For pets?"

"Well, that's just it. There's an auction at the end of the show, and you never know what the buyer will do with your prize animal. Maybe use it for breeding. Maybe for eating."

"Really?" No more grin.

No "duh."

"I raised a shoat the next year. You know, a little pig. Grew to be a big pig." There was probably a picture around somewhere. Lily had half a mind to go looking for it. That was the half that made her smile. "Made a good profit on that guy."

"What was his name?"

"I learned my lesson about naming 4-H projects. I called him Pig. Grandpa called him Bacon. Said that was a 4-H project he could really sink his teeth into. Threatened to bid on him."

"Did he?"

"I didn't stay around for the auction that year. I learned lots of good lessons in 4-H." She was still smiling as she watched Iris reach for a black case on one of the other shelves. "That's my clarinet. I was in band. When we get you enrolled in school, you can—"

Iris opened the case and lifted the instrument from its blue nest. "I'm not gonna join any Lowdown school band, Mom."

"You'll be going to Hilo Consolidated. Two districts merged—High Water and Lowdown. Let me see that." Lily welcomed the familiar weight of the instrument. "You'll be a Hilo Hawk. You soar high up." She put the mouthpiece to her lips and actually got the thing to tweedle. "You dive low down." Yes, she remembered how to sound a low note. The sound made her laugh. "It's poetry in motion."

"You never told me you could play the clarinet."

"It's not my best talent. I'm more of a…" Lily

put the instrument back in the case. She was feeling a little cocky now. "Your mama's not a play-uh."

"Then why do I have to be?"

"You don't." Lily sat down on the single bed. "If I could've kept one piece of furniture, it would have been the piano. You're getting to be so good." With a forefinger she traced a rose on the coverlet. "We used to have one here, but I'm sure your grandfather got rid of it. He's not a music lover."

"Why haven't I seen any pictures of you as a kid until now, Mom?" Iris had taken one of the yearbooks down from the bookshelf. "I was starting to think there aren't any. Like maybe cell phones didn't have cameras back in your day."

"I wouldn't know. I didn't have a cell phone until, I don't know, after you were born."

"But you did have cameras, right?"

"Your grandfather wasn't much of a photographer."

"Well, *somebody* took pictures of you, and you didn't even take any of them with you when you left home." Iris scanned the room. "And here they are, like some kind of ode to Lily Reardon."

"An ode is a—"

"Poem, I know. And this all seems very poetic—your father keeping this room the way you left it. Are you surprised?"

Lily shook her head and shrugged, one gesture cancelling the other out. Surprised? Maybe a little. Did it mean anything? "I guess he had no use for the room. No need to clear it out."

But you didn't frame the pictures, Lily. Who do you suppose did?

"You sure you don't want to keep your room?" Iris asked. "I can use the guest room."

"You just want the double bed." Lily smiled affectionately. "And it's the *spare* room. For spare people."

"Who would be guests. Seems like he'd let Jack use the extra room."

Lily shrugged. "Jack isn't a guest. He's an employee, and he has his own place."

"Yeah, but it's a horse trailer."

"Which is clearly what works for him."

Iris spread her arms dramatically. "Omigod, he is *such* a hottie."

"Iris!" *Good Lord, where has my child gone?*

"Just sayin'. It doesn't hurt to look, does it?"

"It's just that your last hottie was a baby-faced singer with a moppet haircut."

"He spikes his hair now."

"Cowboys don't spike their hair."

"I'm not looking at hair anymore. I've moved on. Speaking of which…" Iris glanced toward the open door. "Hey, Grandpa, is it okay if I change the posters?"

"That's up to you and your mom." Mike braced his forearm against the door frame. "We've got some supper out here, girls. Care to join us?"

"Dad, you don't have to—"

"Mostly cold cuts and leftovers," he said.

"*Us,* Mom," Iris whispered to her mother, flashing a smile. "He said *us.* There's a guest."

"Just Jack and me. Room for two more." He dropped his arm to his side. He looked uneasy, as though he were the visitor. "I cleared off the dining room table and set four places."

"I'm totally famished," Iris said, all breathless teenager.

"Famished," Lily echoed quietly, slipping her daughter a skeptical glance.

Iris answered her mother with a perfunctory smile. "Totally."

The table wasn't quite clear, but it was long enough to accommodate stacks of magazines and paperwork at the far end and still give them plenty of room to eat. Lily recognized the red vinyl place mats with the bandanna pattern, and the plates with the apples on them hadn't changed, either. She doubted he put them out every day. The little table in the kitchen was only big enough for two, but that was the one she and her father had always used after her mother left. That and the plastic plates and whatever utensils happened to be in the drainer.

"Cold drinks in the fridge. Everything else is…" Mike gestured toward the kitchen. "Pop and iced tea. Pretty much all we carry this time of day. But I can make coffee."

"So can I, Dad. Iced tea sounds good."

"Jack's getting cleaned up." He waved his hand toward the table. "Have a seat and dig in."

"Oh, no, we'll wait for Jack," Iris said, even as she followed the first half of the invitation.

Lily offered her daughter a smile, props for minding her manners. Her father had always been a stickler for good manners.

Tense silence took over, disrupted only by the sounds of Mike drinking. Water. He gulped it down—always had—three thunderous gulps, just so you knew he was there at the head of the table. Lily adjusted the position of the fork her dad had placed beside her plate as she glanced furtively across at Iris, who was fooling with something beneath the edge of the table. *No toys at the table.* Who would say it first?

The sound of booted footsteps brought three heads up in unison.

Jack stopped short of the table, swept off his cowboy hat and bowed his head. And yes, he *was* a hottie. Black hair—watered down a bit, if Lily wasn't mistaken—square chin, full lips, broad shoulders, working man's hands gripping the brim of what some women might say was the best kind of hat a man could wear.

Mike laughed. "Hell, man, take a seat."

Jack glanced over at Lily. Hard to tell, but she was pretty sure he was blushing. Iris had been so right. The man was easy on the eyes.

And the innocent look in *his* eyes right now was utterly charming. "Thought I was interrupting a prayer or something."

"More like you answered it," Mike said. "Nobody wants to start without you."

"I thought you said cowboys didn't spike their hair, Mom." *Iris, Iris, Iris.* She slipped her phone—what else could it be?—into the pocket of her jeans. "What do you use? Gel or spray?"

"Water. It's called hat hair, and I was trying to…" Jack raked his hand through his thick wet hair. He glanced at Lily and smiled. "Should I go out and come in again?"

"Oh, no," she said. "We're glad you're here."

Chapter Two

Jack studied the back side of the barn roof, mentally calculating the square footage of the section that had yet to be resurfaced. Mike was strictly a do-it-yourselfer, but there was no way Jack was letting him get up there. It had been at least two years since the front and nearly two-thirds of the back had been covered with galvanized steel roofing. Jack remembered feeling relieved when Mike hadn't asked if he was available to add the roofing job to his schedule. He would have had to say no, and back then it might not have been too hard. Mike had two whole lungs back then.

It probably wouldn't take Jack too long to finish the job if Mike would get him the supplies. Since Mike's surgery, Jack had offered more than once. *Hinted,* more like. Jack didn't have to go looking for work. If there were thirty hours in a day he could easily fill every one of them with jobs he would enjoy, which didn't include roofing. Mike was the only person on God's green earth he would even consider doing that kind of work for. But you didn't offer to help Mike do anything he hadn't hired you for. You might get away with quietly doing something he hadn't asked for, but if he noticed, he would for sure try to pay you for your time. Jack had half a mind to buy the materials himself—sure would be nice to plug up the leaks—but he hadn't figured out a way to apply sheets of metal to a roof without making any noise.

On the ground, sitting close to his right boot, Hula roused herself, pricking her envelope-flap ears. The dog's nose was like an arrow, and Jack's glance followed her direction. It was a moment before he heard footsteps, another before Mike rounded the corner of the barn. He looked tired, and he was clearly trying hard to hide some new pain that had him gimping lately.

He gave Hula a leathery hand to sniff, patted her head, hitched up jeans that were already riding too high, looked up at the roof and folded his arms over his withering chest. "I'm gonna get to that this spring for sure."

"After we finish calving." Jack followed Mike's lead, and the two men stood side by side, arms folded, eyeing the barn roof.

"Absolutely. I'll have plenty of time then. Before it gets too hot. I'm countin' on you to help me with calving."

"You've got me. First on my list. Whenever things get slow here, I've got Jensen and Corey on there, too, but you know you come first."

"You ever thought about taking on a partner?"

"You lookin' for work?" Jack grinned as he adjusted the brim of his hat against the sun. "If I ever thought about it, which I haven't, I don't know too many other men I'd take on."

"How about women?" Mike slid him a straight-faced glance. "Just kidding."

"You got one in mind?"

"If you ever decided to expand, you'd want to go equal opportunity." Mike was back to studying the roof. He lifted a shoulder. "A woman can cowboy as good as a man."

"She's trained for teaching. That's about as good as it gets, I'd say. Lots of schools out here have trouble hangin' on to good teachers. But cowboy like a man?" Jack shook his head. "I don't think so."

"I didn't say *like*. I said just as good. Tell you what, Jack, my girl can *ride*."

"When was the last time you said that to *her?*"

"I don't know. Maybe never." Mike slid one hand down the side of his left thigh and rubbed. "She didn't need to be told. She knew what she could do, and she did it."

"What's going on with your leg?"

"It's gettin' old, just like the rest of me."

Jack adjusted his hat again. "Did you skip your checkup again?"

"No. I did not. And if I needed a secretary I wouldn't hire a cowboy."

"So you finally kept an appointment."

"Yeah, yeah, yeah, I got it done."

"And?"

"They tell me I'm gettin' old." Mike turned, hands on his nonexistent hips, a scowl on his leathery face. "Patch, patch, patch. You just wait, boy. It ain't pretty."

"Trying to imagine you looking pretty," Jack said after a moment's study.

"I never turned female heads the way you do, but I did all right. Lily's mother was a real beauty. You can tell, can't you, just lookin' at my two girls?"

"Sure can. Just so I don't put my foot in it, did you ever tell Lily about your surgery?"

"Hell, no. The docs took care of it. Chopped

that sucker out, sewed me up, good to go." Mike gave a flat-handed wipe-away gesture, folded his arms and turned away again. "So now you've got your answers. Yes, I saw the doctor, and no, I don't talk to nobody but her about my innards. If you hadn't hung around the hospital that time like you were waitin' for spare parts, I wouldn't be havin' this conversation with *you,* neither."

"Her?" Jack grinned. "I never met your doctor. Man, you *are* equal opportunity."

"She's gentle. The one who took the knife to my lung was a man. I told him, leave no stone unturned, take no prisoners, just kill the bastard. And he did. And I don't plan on ever seein' that man again." His thin lips stretched into a wistful smile, momentarily erasing the creases around his mouth. "My regular doctor's a woman. Early forties, nice voice, good hands, laughs easy."

"Surprised you'd ever put off going to see her."

"You maybe haven't noticed, but my charm is limited. I gotta save it up." Mike grinned, raising his eyebrows. "I know what I'm doin'."

"Knowing and doing are two different things." Jack lifted his gaze. "I could finish this roof in a day if I knew how you wanted it done."

"Take you three days at least. We could do it together in a day."

"All right. Order up the materials." Jack looked

down at his boss. "*Today,* Mike. Those calves start dropping, we need a dry barn."

"If I didn't know better, I'd say you were trying to make work for yourself."

"And if you said it I'd take offense, so it's a good thing you know better." Jack tapped Mike's shoulder with the back of his hand. "Have we got a plan? 'Cause I've got things to do."

"You're not on my clock today."

"What clock? I didn't say I had *work* to do. I said *things*."

"Messin' with horses?"

"Messin' with your daughter." He allowed a two-count hush. "And horses."

Jack grinned, and Mike gave him a watch-it-kid look, which was just what Jack was aiming for. He wasn't messing with anybody except Mike, who needed a little poking every so often. He was the kind of guy who thrived when push came to shove, and Jack wanted him to thrive. Wanted him to keep on shoving until it was time to shove off. If Mike felt better keeping people in the dark, so be it. Jack had eyes like a cat.

"So you're taking Lily for a ride?"

"Might be the other way around. *She* asked *me*."

"Did she, now."

"Asked what kind of horses you're keeping around these days. Did I know of any she could start Iris on? Did I have time to take a ride with her and show her where the rest of the horses are?" He chuckled. "Shouldn't've said that in front of Iris. They were heading out to get her enrolled in school, and the girl was already looking to put it off. Her mom was having none of that, so off they went."

"Did Lily ask about her mare?"

Jack frowned.

"Pretty little palomino." Mike glanced away, guiltylike. "I sold her. Lily left, and I just closed all the doors."

"Water under the bridge, Mike. You can always get her another horse."

"Not like that one. Lily raised her, trained her, showed her."

"She can do that again."

"They won't be here that long. She'll get things straightened around real quick. That's the way she is. No grass growing under that girl's feet." Mike stepped back. The plan for the roof had been made. He gazed off in the direction of his pastures. "You'd better get a move on, check those cows."

"Did that first thing. Nothin' yet. Thought I'd head over to the Corey place. Calves are startin' to drop over there."

"I was thinkin' I might need you here." Mike

nodded toward a distant ridge. "Bring them cows in closer."

"I did that last week. They're right over the hill, Mike. You want me to move them into the horse paddock?" The question was meant to make a point, not call for an answer. The two-acre horse paddock was in close but far out of the question. The cows needed space. They were fine where they were for now. "What else you got? I ain't gonna stand around."

"Not even if I pay you for it?" Jack returned a level stare. Mike knew better, so he sighed, surrendering with a chuckle. "Okay, I need you here because I'm...gonna order up the roofing materials." He lifted one shoulder. "And go to a meeting."

"Fair enough."

"Hell, you don't need me to tell you what to do, Jack. You know this operation as well as I do. I don't worry about you standing around."

"Get the hell going, then."

Jack turned away smiling. Mike was big on meetings. The grass-fed cattle co-op he'd started kept him pretty busy these days, and keeping his mind busy was good for Mike's health. That and staying off the bottle. Mike was still a step ahead of the devil in that regard. Jack would know if he wasn't. He knew all the signs. To each his own struggle, Jack figured, but if Mike went down,

Jack would know the reason why. And he would return Mike's many favors, try to be his good neighbor. If it hadn't been for Mike, Jack wouldn't even know what that meant.

With his morning chores done, Jack had already put in what most people would call a day's work, but he would have more work and another paycheck coming if he went over later and spent the afternoon at the Corey ranch. Corey was a friend of Mike's. It was a neighborly friendship, but it was also a business association. Jack didn't know much about either kind. He knew cousins and pals, and he'd walked away from some of each. Had to. It was the only way he could make any sense of who he really was or could become.

He remembered turning off the road the first time he'd followed the arrow on the sign. *Lowdown, Montana. Population: 352, Give or Take a Few.* He'd figured on taking a few. Up to that point, sobriety hadn't been all it was cracked up to be. He'd been out of work for three months and sober the whole damn time. So he'd taken that good turn, then done another for a lonely old man, and he'd been rewarded with steady work, a secure place to park and a new kind of friend.

Jack upended the wheelbarrow at the edge of the compost pile and caught himself checking the approach as he reversed the wheel. He was looking for a little red Chevy.

Didn't mean anything. People who lived out in the country always looked for cars. It was a rare enough sight. He could still hear his grandfather calling out *Car comin'!* from the yard. *Footer,* he would hollered if someone walked into sight, or *two-footer* if it was a couple, *rider* for a horseman. But the approach of a vehicle brought curious faces to windows and opened doors. Footers and riders didn't take you anywhere. Drivers just might.

But Jack was looking for something more than just a car today. A pretty face, a soft voice, a sassy smile. Mike's daughter was the complete package. Her interest in looking at horses made her even more interesting. They would have something to talk about besides the big city, which he knew nothing about. Anything else he could think of offhand was bound to destroy the zone defense he'd learned to play pretty well. *Comfort* zone.

But *she* had asked *him* to go riding. And horses always worked for Jack. He'd always been a good hand, even when everything else was slipping through his fingers. To hear Mike tell it, his daughter was a fair hand herself, not to mention a good student, good teacher, good cook, good mother, good looking—hell, you could zone out, tune back in and Mike would still be talking about Lily. But now that he'd met her, Jack wouldn't be zoning out anymore.

She'd given him her name, caught his eye, and he'd been damn grateful for the shelter of his hat brim. Felt like he'd touched a live electrical wire. Crazy. First time he'd felt that kind of sensation minus a power source. Unless that's what she was.

Damn, what was he? Sixteen?

Hula wheeled right along with him, sticking to his side through every move. That was a herding dog for you. The only true partner Jack had taken on since his divorce. She'd started out pretty useless—the runt of Mike's Catahoula Leopard Dog's last litter. Old Dancer had been devoted to Mike the same way Hula was to Jack. The two men had given her a proper burial under a big old gnarled cottonwood near the river. For Mike the dog had been irreplaceable. He'd gotten a nice chunk of change for the pick of the litter, then sold the rest except for little Hula. If Jack hadn't known better, he would have accused Mike of saving her for him. The old man didn't want to keep the pup for himself, but he couldn't send her away, either.

Jack stored the wheelbarrow in the barn and surveyed the interior, alley to loft to rafters. The sun was leaking through the roof big-time. Nothing he could do about leaks of any kind without roofing. That metal sheeting was damn good stuff. Jack had built a simple pole barn on his own place years ago, back when he'd had his own place. He could do it again, better this time. Build it bigger and better in half the time, now that he knew what he was doing.

You know what your problem is, Jack? You're not happy unless you're on the move. I don't know where you want to be, but I know it isn't here.

Even before they were married, Edie's nickname for him had been Lonesome. She said he'd called her once and claimed he was "real lonesome." He didn't remember doing it, but since it sounded like beer talk, he took her word for it. They'd known each other since they were kids, and they weren't much more than that when they'd gotten married. Edie had been ready for marriage; Jack was okay with it. They'd had two sweet years with lots of laughs, two salty years with plenty of tears, two sour years with silence, and in the middle of it all they'd had two babies. Now that they were friends again she was letting him see the kids.

He didn't mind being alone, and he didn't think of himself as the lonesome cowboy type. He'd always kept to himself on the inside even when he'd been a big party boy on the outside. It had seemed like a good combination—real manly— but it hadn't made him a good husband. Maybe he wasn't husband material. The party boy had become a sober man, but he'd lost most of what he'd had in the process, and he was keeping the rest to himself. Safer that way. For everybody.

Still, the sound of a car in desperate need of a tune-up had him turning toward the open barn door. Hula was standing at attention, ready to sound her warning if he would allow. Yeah, the car sounded as if it was still chewing on the bones of its last victim, but it carried a person of interest. The good kind. He stepped outside into the sunlight.

"Are we still on?" Lily asked as she strode purposefully in his direction, a flirty sparkle alight in her eyes.

She wore tall leather boots with chunky two-inch heels—the kind that couldn't be easy to walk in but sure as hell looked good on a woman—and a tan wool coat that hit her about mid-thigh, showing off some of her black skirt. She smiled as she reached back and set her hair free. Her hand came away with a big brown clip, and her reddish-brown hair unfurled like a flag lifted on the crisp March breeze.

He couldn't find the voice to ask *On what?*

"You were going to show me the horses, remember?"

"Sure," he said. "I'll round up a couple of saddle horses while you..."

"Get changed." She tucked the clip in her coat pocket. "As long as I was going to be at the school, I figured it wouldn't hurt to go looking the part. And guess what. They *do* need subs. It doesn't pay very well, but it's a start." She glanced down at Hula. "Yours?"

"Yeah, she's—"

"Is it okay to pet her?"

"Sure."

"I always make sure." She knew enough to let the dog sniff her hand first. Hula's gyrating tail put Lily at the top of the smells-good chart. "What's her name? She looks like a Catahoula. I had one once. Is she good with kids?" She bent her knees and started sinking toward eye-level with the dog, but she turned her ankle.

Hula jumped back, and Jack caught Lily before she toppled.

"Oops!" She looked up and surprised him with a quick laugh. "Nice save. Thanks." He steadied her while she reset her feet, and then she made kissing noises at the dog, offering her hand again. Hula moved back in, and there was a whole lot of licking and giggling and scratching and petting.

Jack felt a little cheated.

"She's not around kids that much, but she's never offered them any trouble. She's at her best with cattle. And me." Lily stood up smiling, wiping the dog slobber off her chin with the back of her hand. "And now you."

"Iris has always wanted a dog, but I wouldn't

have one in the city." Hula whined for another pat on the head, and she got it. "Aw, you're such a love." Jack would have given the dog a warning, but he didn't want to wipe away whatever points his gallant catch might have gained him. "What's her name?" Lily asked again.

"Hula." He shrugged diffidently. "My daughter named her."

"Your daughter? How old is she?"

"She's just about Iris's age. Two kids," he added. Hadn't been asked, but he was unwilling to leave anyone out. "My boy is eleven."

"You didn't mention children last night."

"Nobody asked." Still hadn't, but for some reason he felt like getting some facts out. "I've been married. I'm not now."

"I never was. As I'm sure my father's told you." Her eyes challenged him for a denial, but then she let him off the hook with a quick shrug. "Which is probably why we kept the conversation to a minimum last night."

"About a week ago Mike mentioned you might be moving back home, you and your daughter. Said you and her father weren't together." Now they were even. She knew as much as he did. "That's about it."

"I didn't give him much notice. *My* father, not Iris's. Her father and I were never together, really. I mean, we were, but…" She shook her head, made a funny little sound as though they were still talking about kids other than themselves. "Teenagers. What're you gonna do, huh?"

"You tell me. Being one is a real rush. Watching your kid turn into one…"

"Scary." She glanced past him toward the barn. "You sure you have time?"

"Oh, yeah. Long as we ride through the cows on our way to look at the horses."

"I'll go change. Just be a minute."

"No rush." They looked at each other and laughed. "You left all this behind, right? Ended up east of here, about…what? Six, seven hundred miles?"

"Something like that."

"Time's nothing here. But daylight?" He flashed her a wink and a smile. "Now that's something you don't wanna burn."

When Lily stepped out the back door she found Jack half sitting on the hood of her car with the reins of two saddled sorrels in his gloved hands. She hesitated. Gloves. All she had were a pair of thin stretchy ones she kept in her coat pocket and her heavy-duty mittens. But he was already pushing away from her car, and she wasn't sure how much time their ride would take. And she wanted to save plenty of daylight for Iris.

"Where's Hula?"

"You need a chaperone?" He laughed. "Cows are edgy enough right now without having a dog around."

"I knew that." She gave a quick smile. "Just sticking up for a friend."

"You changed your boots," he said with a pointed glance, and she knew what he was thinking. These boots were navy blue with tan wingtips and fancy stitching to match her favorite show outfit, which she'd found—to her surprise—hanging in the back of her old closet.

"I haven't worn these in years. I've had them since high school." She planted her heel in the dirt and turned her toe up, hoping he would notice that they were broken in and had a few scuffs. She remembered a time when she'd felt pretty damned dazzling wearing her blue boots. "At least they're comfortable."

"I don't know how they do things in the big city, but out here, you find a boot that works for you, you stick with it."

"And don't worry about looking the part?" She took the reins he offered and swung up into the saddle. "Freeedomm!"

His laughter rang out behind her as they urged the two sorrels through their paces and made for the wide-open spaces.

The closer pastures were reserved for calving this time of year, and the size of the bellies on the mostly black white-faced expectant mothers gave proof that the smallest of the pastures would soon be a busy place. For now the cows moved slowly or stood quietly, showing no interest in anything but nibbling last year's grass or soaking up this afternoon's sun.

"The heifers calved out pretty easy this year," Jack told her as the horses wended their way through the herd. "Cows should start dropping their calves any day now."

"Perfect weather for calving. Nice and dry."

She wasn't even missing her gloves, but that was partly because it felt so good to be back on a horse that all she wanted to do was sit on top of the world and enjoy the warmth of fuzzy winter coat, silky mane and muscles not her own working in concert with hers.

"We had an easy winter out here," Jack was saying, and his voice became part of the warmth until he added, "Mike thinks that means we're in for a spring snowstorm."

Lily groaned. "Either that or he thinks we're in for a drought. The weather is one glass that's always half-empty, whatever the forecast." She looked to him for agreement, but he wasn't smiling. She shrugged. "Which is fine, unless he half emptied the glass while he was grumbling about it."

"In his business you're always at the mercy of the weather."

"How long have you been working for him?"

"About seven years."

"Really. That long." She wondered why her father hadn't mentioned his hired help either time he'd visited. Or his switch to raising grass-fed beef, which must have taken a major financial commitment. The Mike Reardon she knew was old school, a cow-calf man whose six-month-old product went to auction in the fall to be "finished" on corn in a Midwestern feedlot. "That kind of job security is hard to come by these days," she said.

"I'm on my own, trading on my experience, just like everyone else."

"And your outstanding reputation." No reaction. She wasn't sure he was listening. "Dad says you're very much in demand."

"You look, you'll find something to do." He might have been talking to himself as he stood in his stirrups and eased his sorrel into a trot, headed down the grassy draw toward a cluster of cows.

Lily picked up her pace behind him. She wasn't sure whether she'd said something wrong, but she knew she wanted to rectify it. She circled the grazing cows from the opposite side, made a mental note of a couple of ear-tag numbers on cows that were bagging up and mentioned them when she met up with Jack.

"Yeah, I noticed those heavies this morning.

Two-forty-two always takes several days baggin' up, but I gotta watch two-ninety. She'll swell all of a sudden like you hooked her to a tank of helium." And then, as though her job search might blow up the same way… "You could probably put together a living, same as me. Start out subbing for schools in several towns. How far are you willing to drive?"

"As far as my car will let me." She laughed. She had helium on the brain now, and she imagined her car as a Mylar balloon. "I wasn't sure it would get us *this* far."

"You want me to take a look at it?"

"Are you a mechanic?"

"Nope. I'm just a cowboy."

"I just meant…is it, like, a sideline?"

He laughed. "You put a whole phone book full of sidelines together, you've got a cowboy."

"You mean you really could fix my car?"

"I don't know. Said I could take a look at it."

"My father used to do all his own engine repairs."

"He still does. I can't offer you his services. I'm offering mine. If I can figure out what's wrong, I'll do what I can to fix it." He nodded toward a cow treading a worn path over a low rise up ahead. "That one's looking for a little privacy."

"You would, too."

"I'd be looking for the painkillers." He glanced

at her and surprised her with a cocky wink. "Or the damn bull."

"Or a safe place where you can get the job done," she said with a smile. "Back to the car…I might just take you up on your offer after I put in a few days of subbing."

"I'll take a look at it tonight."

"If you work on it tonight, you'll have to take either an IOU or a credit card. What'll it be?"

"Neither." He grinned boyishly as he urged his horse to take the hill. Lily's sorrel bounded up the narrow cow path behind him. At the top of the rise he turned to her, still grinning. "I take sweets," he shouted. "Been hearing about those pies you make for seven years now."

"I haven't made one in a while, but since my credit cards aren't worth the plastic they're printed on, the pie is a better bet." They paused, horses side by side, overlooking a hidden draw with a few scrub pines. The lone cow had found a sister-in-waiting. "Are you a gambling man?" she asked.

"If it looks sweet, I always take a chance. If it's only money, hell, driving past the gas station when I'm one notch above Empty is my idea of taking a gamble. Betting the price is going down tomorrow. I do it all the time, just for fun."

"I'll have to try that."

"You're more the tank-half-full kind of woman?"

"You know my father." She downshifted into a gruff tone. "Don't bring that car back here with the gas below half, girl. You go below half, you'd better be stopping at Cenex." She lifted one shoulder as she shifted her voice back up. "I do it all the time now, too, but it isn't fun anymore. I'll have to try thinking of it that way."

"Worse comes to worst, walking is good exercise."

"Then you're the one who's a tank-half-full type."

"I'm one-day-at-a-time on that score." He nodded toward the two cows. "Their day's coming."

"I see the horses," Lily said, pointing toward the fence beyond the cows' little sanctuary. She counted five horses in an array of sizes and colors. "Where's that beautiful paint of yours?"

"Haven't had a chance to turn her out there yet, but she'll be getting a little vacation now till calving's over with. This time next year she'll be a good cow pony." He clucked to his sorrel, and they started down the slope. "Let's get closer. We've got a couple of choices down there for pleasure riding. See that little red roan Appaloosa? He's a nice-size gelding, and he's well-broke."

"These two make a nice matched pair," she said of their mounts.

"This one's the best calf horse I've ever had.

Name's Rusty. That mare is your dad's horse. He calls her Bunny."

"That doesn't sound like Dad." She patted the horse's neck, and Bunny's unusually big ears perked up as if on cue. "But, Grandma, what long ears you have," she recited in a deep, gruff voice that *did* sound like Dad. He was the one who'd read to her every night. She sat up straight, wondering why she'd forgotten that. "My favorite Doctor Seuss story was *Hop on Pop,* and my first 4-H project was a pair of rabbits named Hoppsie and Poppsie."

"Guess that explains where the name came from," Jack said. "He said he wasn't even in the market for a horse, but he bought her because somebody at the sale barn was making fun of her ears."

"She has an easy trot and a smooth canter." She patted the mare's neck again. "You're a nice ride, Bunny."

"Mike says you came up with a good recipe for treating scours back when you were his right-hand girl."

"Not mine. My mother used to make it."

"Well, now it's your recipe. Last one to mix it up gets the credit." He scanned the sky. "If the weather holds, maybe we won't need it this season."

Lily looked up. Herringbone clouds painted over bright blue heaven. "What are the odds?"

"Even, I'd say. But that's only because my bones ain't speaking to me yet. Ask me again in five years."

"Five years? Your bones won't be forecasting the weather that soon. How old are you?

"I'm thirty-five, which is getting up there in cowboy years."

"Old rodeo injuries?"

"One or two. Enough so I gave up on ridin' rough stock. I still do a little roping."

"Like all cowboys. Little of this, little of that. Oh, look!" She pointed to a trio of antelope sailing over the wire fence.

Jack chuckled. "They don't play in Minneapolis?"

"We've got plenty of deer, but no antelope." She glanced at him, and they said *"Pronghorn"* in unison and laughed. And then she added, "Speed goats."

He gave a single nod of approval. "You're homegrown, all right."

"And you?"

"I'm from Lewistown originally. My kids live near Wolf Point. I did some ranching around there a few years back."

"And after that?"

"I signed on at a few places along the Hi-line," he said, speaking of Highway 2, the Route 66 of the North. "Until I figured out how to make the work come to me."

"How do you do that?"

"You hone your salable skills and build your reputation one job at a time. Not too many guys can afford a full-time hand these days. You bring your own horse, your own gear, your own tools, and you do what you're hired to do the way the boss wants it done."

"And they come to you?"

He nodded as he dismounted and opened the gate into another pasture. "I fill up quick, especially this time of year. Members of Mike's co-op, mostly."

"Mike's co-op?"

"For grass-fed beef. Pretty much your dad's baby. He and a couple of his neighbors were just getting it started when I came down here looking for work."

"My dad's baby," she mused. Jack was standing there holding the wire-strung wood swing post that served as a gate, patiently waiting for her to ride through.

"He's pretty proud of that co-op. Been a lot of work, convincing enough ranchers to join and building the market for grass-finished meat, but it's really caught on." He jabbed the bottom of the post into the set post loop, muscling the gate wires taut as he latched the gate shut with another simple wire loop. Then he mounted in one smooth motion, turned to her and smiled. "High Plains Beef. That's the baby's name."

"Never heard of it."

"This is the main *herd of it* right here." With a nod he turned her attention to a rolling pasture dotted with steers grazing on the remains of last summer's grass.

"Clever." She was scanning her father's domain, but her smile was for his hired hand.

"Surprised he hasn't talked your ear off about it."

"That's not his way. He wants the ears on and tuned in because he's *only gonna say this once, girl*."

"That ain't the Mike Reardon I know. Not when he gets started talkin' grass and beef."

"He's always loved those cows, but steers?" She was looking at a pasture full of yearlings. "He stopped running steers when he decided they weren't worth the trouble. He said he was tired of fixing fence."

"Now he's got me to fix the fence." Jack smiled. "You should take in a co-op meeting. What they're doing is pretty interesting. No drugs, no feedlots, just mother's milk and Montana grass. You could get into that, couldn't you? The way nature intended?"

"I'm a natural woman, all right."

They were following the fence line toward the river. This was her favorite part of the ranch, where the expansive grassland gave way to the rugged ridges and draws, outliers of the dramatic Missouri Breaks, where the river had carved out steep bluffs and settled into its winding channel. She had forgotten how much she loved riding in this boundless, uncompromising country.

"Where did you get Hula?" she asked.

"Mike decided I needed a friend."

"She looks like one I had. I didn't have her very long. Dad gave her away." *You can take that bitch home with you,* he'd told one of the neighbors who'd come over for branding. The work was done, and the beer was flowing. *Like all females, she got pregnant. You take all them squealin' mongrel pups, too. There's one for each of your boys.* "Her name was Dancer."

"Mike had Dancer when I came to work for him. Hula's one of her pups."

"Must have been a different Dancer. Hula's purebred, isn't she?"

"I never asked. She was the runt of Dancer's last litter."

It was hard to believe his dog's mother could have been *her* Dancer. She'd been given the dog as a pup, and she'd been allowed to keep it even though her father never seemed to want dogs around, especially after her mother had left. They'd argued over keeping pets. He'd said animals didn't belong in the house. Her mother used to bring home a kitten in a box or a bird in a cage and say it was for Lily, that Lily would take care of it. Every disagreement between her parents had always included at least one exchange about bringing animals in the house. *I wasn't born in a barn,* Dad would say quietly, as though he were trying to dispel a nasty rumor.

But Dancer had been a gift from another rancher—somebody her father liked—which was, she'd believed, the real reason the dog was allowed to stay.

For a while.

She turned to find Jack watching her.

"Let's take a ride over by the river," he said.

Lily wanted more than a ride. She wanted a race. She wanted the wind to blow through the hard-edged memories, blur them a little, soften them so her mind wouldn't get hung up on them at every turn. Jack obliged her. He didn't push, but he let his mount gallop nose to nose with hers. He could have surged ahead, but he didn't. He was having a good time with her, and it pleased her to be indulged this way.

They reined in near a huge bare-branch cottonwood growing a few yards from the riverbank. The river was swollen with early spring runoff, running swiftly, carving another year's notch into the steep cut bank on the far side of the channel. The vibrant blue sky made a breathtaking contrast to the sameness of pale clay-colored water, tree and cut bank. A few sprigs of evergreen high at the top of the sandstone bluff hinted of the color that would—with sunshine and some precipitation—come in a few weeks.

It was one of Lily's favorite places on the ranch. Isolated from human traffic and unchanged by anything but the flow of time and water, it was a serene piece of earth. A rarity.

Jack dismounted. Wordlessly she followed his lead, horse at her shoulder, and realized that something had changed since she'd been here last. Jack stood looking down at a pile of red rock.

"When I bring Hula out here, she comes right over and sniffs around. I don't think she can smell anything anymore, but she knows."

"What's there?"

"Dancer."

Lily stared at the loosely arranged rock pyramid. "Here? You buried her all the way out here?"

"This is where your dad wanted her. Had to have a marker, he said, something special. I hauled every one of those rocks half a mile or more."

"You couldn't find anything closer? That's just a pile of rock that…" She bent to examine the array of quartzite rocks that looked as if they'd been split with a mallet. She glanced up. "…didn't come from around here. This is sandstone country."

"That's fire-cracked rock. You've got an old tipi ring a little ways down river."

"Really? How do you know?"

"Little hobby of mine. I spend a lot of time riding around what used to be buffalo country. You find telltale signs like what you noticed, rock that's not natural to the area." He squatted on his heels next to her. "The only way this kind of rock gets cracked like this is if somebody heats it up and then it cools off quick. They were used to boil water, pit-roast meat. Bigger stones were probably rolled into a sweat lodge."

"By your ancestors?"

"Probably back further than that. We call them First People. My people came later. Métis. Mixed-bloods—European trappers and Cree, maybe some Chippewa or Sioux. We're kinda gypsy-like."

Lily smiled. "That's what Dad said when Iris asked about your trailer. I thought he was being… you know. *Dad.*"

"I suppose he was." He lifted one shoulder. "I kid him about what he calls his Irish roots.

No matter where he puts 'em down, they sprout spuds."

"Where?" Lily challenged. "He'll be the first to tell you he's no farmer."

"He puts in a garden every spring."

"That's *my* job. Or was." She shook her head, amazed. "What does he grow? He hates vegetables."

"He gives most of it away. Hell, I like vegetables." He grinned. "Especially spuds."

"Grass-fed steak and homegrown potatoes." She laughed. "My mother was a fan of Big Macs and French fries. I didn't know that until I went to Minneapolis to live with her."

Her smile dissolved. Her mother was the last subject she'd meant to mention in the last place her mother would want to be mentioned. She glanced at Jack. He knew. He lowered his gaze to the marker and let her take the conversation where she would.

"First People," she mused as she squatted to take a closer look at the cracked rocks. "Should you be disturbing a tipi ring?"

He chuckled. It was a nice sound, somehow restorative. "You want me to haul these back?"

"I don't know. I just wondered. They're more yours than mine."

"I don't think either one of us has much claim. The people who put them there would probably get a good laugh over not disturbing them. They hauled them there in the first place." He squatted across from her, forearms resting across his knees. "Probably get another laugh over making a burial marker for a dog."

"I wonder if it's my Dancer."

"Mike used to breed her to a Catahoula over in Havre. Sold the pups from that last litter, 'cept for her. Kept her for me, I guess."

"He must've thought you needed a friend." Lily shook her head, nonplussed. "And he made sure you got one."

"We're good together. I fill her bowl every night, and she gets me up every morning before daybreak."

"I wanted to train Dancer to herd cattle," she recalled. Whatever it took to keep her, she'd promised. But it hadn't mattered.

"They're bred for it. I'd never worked with a dog before, so Hula had to train me in a little bit."

"Hula dancer. I'm picturing her wiggling her hips."

"She does. She'll dance for you next time she sees you. Any friend of mine is a friend of Hula's." He stood slowly. "Iris should be fine around her."

Lily shot to her feet, gasping her daughter's name. "What time is it? What time does the bus get here? I told her I'd be waiting at the gate."

"If you're not, the bus will take her to the door."

"But I *said* I'd—" She mounted her horse. "Let's ride, cowboy."

Chapter Three

Lily reveled in the cool wind in her hair and the heated power of the horse beneath her. She glanced at the sorrel galloping beside her and the man riding as smoothly as she did. They exchanged knowing smiles. *This is the only way to fly.*

They were riding the fence line along the right-of-way. A few yards away the yellow bus pulled even with them. The driver gave a two-fingered wave without lifting his hand from the steering wheel, and Jack waved back. It would be a photo finish at the Rocking R gate.

But an old black pickup was already parked on

the cattle guard, waiting. Mike emerged just as the bus and the horses converged at the turnoff. Iris clambered down the steps and gave each of her greeters a puzzled look as she adjusted her backpack on her shoulder.

"See you made it home," Mike said.

Iris stared for a minute as the bus pulled away. She looked as though she didn't know whether to laugh or cry. She chose the former.

Belatedly, the adults joined in.

"Way to embarrass me in front of the whole bus," Iris said as the four of them watched the school bus rumble down the two-lane highway.

But she was smiling when she turned around and looked up at Lily and Jack, both tall in the saddle, while Iris, having gathered a crowd, was small but mighty on the ground. "Where's a camera when you need one?" she said, sassy as pepper sauce. "I have a real posse."

"I take it Hilo's not half-bad," Lily said.

"Almost half, maybe just a hair under." Iris scowled at her mom. "I thought you were going to wait for me to go riding."

"Jack took me out to see the horses." Lily glanced at her father, who was leaning against the hood of his pickup. "I was hoping you still had Juniper."

"Phil Jensen was after that horse for his girl

soon as he heard you'd gone to live with your mother. I told him if you came back…" He shifted his weight gingerly, going easy on his left side. "You know, I guess I owe you for that horse."

Owed her for the horse? It was an odd thought. Back when she was a kid the horse had been her pride and joy, but overnight she'd stopped being a kid. She'd taken a bus to Minnesota and left her childhood in Montana.

"What did you get for her?" Lily asked.

"What would you have asked?"

"I wouldn't have sold her." Lily dismissed the topic with a smile for her daughter and a pat on the neck for her mount. "I think we could start you on this one. Her name is Bunny, and she's big, but she's gentle. Grandpa rides her." She glanced back at her father. "Right, Dad?"

"Not lately, but she's always taken good care of me when I did."

"Just to start," Lily said. "Grandpa gets his horse back as soon as Jack finds your personal match."

"Is he working on a match for you?" Iris had mischief in her eyes.

Lily fired mischief right back. "Maybe."

"Grandpa doesn't need a horse," Mike said. "I've never been much of a horseman. That mare is yours now, you girls. The horses are mostly Jack's these days anyway. Far as I'm concerned—"

"Far as I'm concerned, you need to stop trying to give your stuff away," Jack said.

"Far as *I'm* concerned, anybody wants to give me a horse, I'll take it," Iris said. All smiles and eyes alight, she looked up at Lily and clapped her hands, goody-goody style. "We have a horse! I forgive you for going riding without me, but now it's my turn."

"Right after supper," Lily said. "How was school?"

"It was school. On a very small scale." Iris adjusted the backpack strap on her shoulder with one hand and planted the other one on her hip. "Ask me if I learned anything."

"I thought I'd save that question for the end of the week."

But when Iris was ready with an answer, she didn't need a question.

"I learned that you don't go riding down the road less traveled when you have promises to keep." She glanced at Jack, beaming. "Robert Frost."

"That's two poems," Lily said. She had some smarts to show off, too.

"That's right, a twofer. And, speaking of promises—because that's what the discussion in class was about—you lose your thanks when you promise and delay. You know what that's from?" Iris gave her mother two seconds to answer. "Got'cha. Proverbs. I wrote that one down."

"Sounds as though Hilo Consolidated already has a good English teacher."

"She seems okay." Iris lowered her backpack to the ground. "So how about it? Let me ride your horse back to the house, Mom. You ride back with Grandpa."

"*I'll* ride with Grandpa." Jack signaled Lily as he dismounted. "Trade with me."

She muttered, "Are you sure?" even as she complied. It surprised her, how wobbly her legs felt. It surprised her even more, how willing she was.

Jack leaned closer to Lily's ear and whispered, "Take the reins, Mom," as he traded with her.

He nodded to Iris. "You ever had a leg up?"

"Uh…"

Lily watched with a loving smile as Iris followed Jack's instructions to the letter. The look in her eyes when she landed in the saddle and saw Big Sky Country for the first time from the back of a horse was priceless. Lily felt like a kid again and a mother, both at the same time. Passing the torch.

"If you want to trade places with me along the way, give us a high sign," Jack told Iris after he'd adjusted the length of her stirrups and given her a few pointers. "We'll follow along."

Iris grinned. "Don't be tailgating."

Jack chuckled as he jumped into the pickup's passenger seat. The girl was just as quick as his Becky and twice as bold. But he couldn't help enjoying a little adolescent sass. He'd seen for himself how a feisty coming-teenager could check back into her soon-to-be-history little-girl self in a heartbeat.

And he knew exactly what those moments did to a parent's heartbeat.

"Things sure are gonna be different around here," Mike said.

"Women, huh? Who knows what they're talking about half the time?"

"You sure got their attention." Mike gave Jack a pointed glance.

"I'm the novelty." More like the neutral zone, Jack thought, which for him was a novelty. The neutral zone was somewhere in the middle. When it came to family ties, he'd long been a loose end. "That girl is gonna be sore. This is what you call seat-of-the-pants education."

"It's not Iris's seat you're eyeing."

"Course not." Jack stared through the windshield and grinned. "I could watch that woman ride all day long."

"And during calving season you can even get paid for it. Gonna really need you this year."

"You're making it damn hard to squeeze Jensen and Corey into my schedule."

"Don't see how you can, boy. Maybe you oughta snuff out that end of your candle and be done with it."

Jack's smile wilted. He was making a damn good living as a day worker, best he'd ever done, if *living* was all about dollars and cents. And his business depended on his capacity to cobble together several sources of part-time wages to make up a full-time job. He'd worked hard to build his reputation. He was steady. He was reliable. His word was good.

And Mike's health was not.

Jack cared deeply for the man. When the time came, he was the kind of man who would want to die with his boots on, and Jack would be there to make sure those boots were right where Mike wanted them.

He wasn't sure how he was going to take care of the Rocking R's growing needs and still keep his business intact, but he would come up with something. A few more hours in the day, maybe.

Meanwhile Jack was going to sit down to supper at a real table with real people whenever he got the chance. He'd almost forgotten that food was more than something you had to get down so you could get going again. There was actually a taste to it, and the sound of voices around the table somehow boosted all the flavors.

Lily had put together a simple meal, and Iris had set the table up family style—serving bowls instead of pots, and salt and pepper in little rooster and hen shakers instead of a round box and a square tin.

"You notice I didn't fall off once," Iris boasted. "It was bouncier than I thought it would be, but you get used to it, right?"

"That was your first horseback ride?" Jack asked.

"Pretty much."

Jack glanced at the window. "We'll have a good hour's worth of daylight after we get cleaned up here if you want a few pointers. Your mom's gonna be your best teacher, but I can sure help out."

"Her mom will be soaking in the bathtub as soon as we get cleaned up here," Lily said as she lined the edge of her knife up on her ham.

"Oh, no, you won't," Iris said. "Not until they turn off the daylight. I'm ready for my close-up riding lesson. Out there in the big corral, right, Jack?"

"It was just a suggestion." Which he wished he could take back.

"Let's see…" Lily lifted her gaze to the frosted-glass ceiling light above the table. "Ease my aching keester or risk losing my kid's thanks. Hmm, pain in the keester, pain in the neck, pain in the keester, pain in the…" She counted her options with the point of her knife. "Okay, but mother-daughter appreciation is a cradle-to-grave proposition. When I'm old and all my pain leads to a cane, you remember you're my only child."

"Yes!" Iris gave a fork-filled fist pump.

Lily got her glow on, all love-my-baby smiles. Jack couldn't help but smile with her even if he was feeling a little pinch inside his chest. *A daughter's a daughter the rest of her life.* First time he'd heard the saying, he'd thought it was a given. Not a gift, but a dyed-in-the-DNA given for the father of a little girl. But if he'd voiced his thoughts at the time, he would have had no real idea what he was talking about.

Lily was a full-time mother, and he was…

He was trying to cobble together a few days here and a few hours there to put together some semblance of fatherhood—whatever his former wife and his faraway kids would allow. And Mike? Jack glanced toward the end of the table. His heart went out to the old man, who was studiously poking at his ham steak with his fork.

"Now that you're in a good mood, tell us a little more about school," Lily said. "And remember, Hilo is my alma mater, so fair and balanced, if you please."

"Okay, I did learn something." The corners of Iris's mouth twitched as she reached for the salt and pepper shakers, which she'd already used at least once. "I learned that hooters aren't boobs here. They're people. Like, somebody said, 'A pair of Hooters walked into Bailey's on Saturday.'"

"Hutterites," Lily said. Jack smiled to himself as he reached for his glass of water. "Kind of like Amish."

"Which I found out after the whole lunch table had a good laugh."

"What did you say?"

Iris shrugged. "I wondered if a disembodied… you know, male part, walked in with her."

"That got a laugh?" Lily said, incredulous.

Jack glanced at the other male at the table, but Mike was all about his next bite of ham.

"That and the milk shooting out of Lyle LeBeau's nose. Obviously I didn't say *disembodied male part.* Not to them."

Mike choked on his ham, and Jack bubbled his water.

Lily glanced from one man to the other. *"Don't ask."*

"Don't have to," Mike said.

Lily sighed. "Okay, that was funny."

"Why aren't you laughing, Mom? Is the funny bone connected to the keester bone?" The kid was enjoying the spotlight. "*I'm* not sore at all. Seriously."

"But you *are* funny," Lily said with a smile. "Seriously. Finish up so we can get you back in the saddle."

"What kind of pointers do I need? Stopping and turning? I think my horse was just following yours, because I wasn't really sure how to make him do anything. I was just sitting there bouncing along. Is it always that bouncy? Not that I minded bouncing, but I noticed you weren't bouncing, and I just wondered if—"

Lily laughed. "The sooner you stop talking and start eating, the sooner we can poke you with your first pointer."

The sun would soon drop behind the rugged hills on the western horizon and take its warmth with it. Lily had almost forgotten what *big sky country* meant. You never had to look up. It was all around you—big light, big dark, big color. She took it all in from her perch atop the corral rail, sitting there like a bird flanked by two males of her kind. They'd given takeoff and landing lessons to her daughter, and now they were sitting back, watching her wind down. She was grooming Bunny.

And he was loving it.

"Bailey says he can get the roofing materials delivered next week." From where he stood near Lily's left elbow, Mike seemed to direct the comment to no one in particular.

"That's quick," said Jack, who was on the fence on her other side. "How'd you manage that?"

"Seniority in the co-op. Put the six of us together, we're a big chunk of Bailey's business."

"How'd your meeting go? Are the Tyrees ready to join yet?"

Mike gave a dry chuckle. "Never happen, not as long as the ol' man has the final say. He wants to pump those babies full of growth hormones in the spring and collect his calf check in the fall."

"Should be turning his operation over to his kids pretty soon," Jack said. "Saw him a couple days ago over at the Corey place. He's on his last legs."

"Some of his boots are looking pretty decrepit, too," Lily said, earning a couple of laughs.

"That's my ace in the hole," Mike said. "Told him we could put a picture of that fence in our advertising. Pretty sure I saw a glint in his eye."

"Advertising for what?" Lily asked, smiling at the sight of Iris slipping her arms around Bunny's neck and nuzzling, just the way Lily had done countless times as a kid. Some girls sought comfort food. For others it was comfort horse. The smell was heaven.

"Advertising good meat from healthy, happy, grass-fed steers," her father was saying. "There's a growing market for free-range beef, no feedlot finish. A few of us got together to form this co-op. Separately we're small ranchers, but together we sure can show 'em where the beef is. Six members—can you beat that? *Six*."

Lily stared, completely nonplussed. Not by the enterprise itself, or even the words, but by the voice that sounded like her father's except for the enthusiasm. Who was he? He looked like Mike Reardon—although visibly worse for wear and time—but he sounded different. More alive than he had been fourteen years ago.

"Jack told me a little about the co-op earlier," she said. "I had no idea."

"We've changed up a few things since you left. Guess I didn't say much about it when I saw you last. I wanted you to show me around where *you* lived. You know, tell me about your school, Iris's activities."

"That was, what? Four years ago?"

"Didn't wanna wear out my welcome," Mike said, forcing a chuckle. Lily caught the exchange of looks between her father and Jack. "And I thought maybe you'd pay *me* a visit."

"You never said that."

"I know. I should've. Time gets away, you know?" He paused long enough for someone to agree. No one did. He cleared his throat and filled the silence. "Must have felt funny signing your daughter up at your old school. Hasn't changed much over there."

"Hasn't changed at all." That much Lily could confirm without softening. She took a deep, inhaling breath of relief at the change of subject.

"I was on the school board for a while," Mike said. Another surprise. "When the school needs something new, we get it. Did you ask about jobs?"

"They need subs. I have some forms to fill out. Transcripts to send for. Background check to pass. Cup to pee in." No response. "The last one was a joke."

Mike chuckled. "You had me going there, girl."

"Did the chicken's sense of humor come first, or was it the egg's?" Jack asked, deadpan.

"They sure didn't get it from me," Mike said.

"No, but they're gettin' you to laugh," said Jack. "Seems like I read somewhere that laughter is the best medicine."

"You name it, this guy's read something about it."

Jack turned his attention elsewhere. "You've got a friend now, Iris." He braced one hand on the fence and dropped to the ground. "You can just tell Bunny's feelin' all warm and fuzzy right now," he said as he strode across the corral. "How 'bout you? You feelin' the love?"

"Feeling the fuzziness for sure." She peeled a horsehair mat off the currycomb and held it up for Jack's inspection. "This is number eleven."

"And the shedding is only just beginning. Let's turn her out."

"I could've kept brushing. I mean…" Iris raked her fingers through Bunny's mane. "Yeah. I do feel the love. It's, like, relaxing and kind of Zen-feeling."

"Which means?"

"Bunny knows what it means. Don't you, Bun?" Iris flashed her mother a smile. "Totally and peacefully in the moment, right?"

Lily nodded.

"You're a natural-born horse person, all right," Jack said.

Lily took a closer look at the face in the mirror as she rinsed her toothbrush. She'd gotten some sun. Pink nose, pink cheeks, eyes aglow—her natural radiance was back, and all it had taken was a few hours in the saddle.

"Didn't it feel good to take a bath instead of a shower after all that riding?" Lily called, then took the muffled sound coming from her old bedroom to be an affirmative. "Do you have your clothes all ready for tomorrow?"

No sound.

"Five-thirty comes early, honey."

Again no sound. Five-thirty should have elicited adolescent horror.

Lily stepped across the hall and peeked around the half-open door. Iris had fallen asleep on top of Grandma Reardon's crazy quilt, the one Lily had always carefully folded down to the foot of the bed first thing in her nightly ritual. The quilt would be Iris's now, but Lily would insist that she take care of it. Tomorrow. For now she would cover her little girl with the soft blanket she'd returned to for comfort ever since she'd first ventured across a room on her own two feet. For good measure she added the pink-and-green granny-squares afghan that had been her first and last crochet project.

And then she slipped outside, tipped her head back and drank in the night sky.

She knew it was no accident that the light was on in the barn, but even so, she told herself it might be and that she should make sure. Hula trotted over to check her out but stopped short at the sound of her master's whistle. Lily extended her hand palm up as she sank into a squat and made a kissing sound. She had nothing to offer but a pat, but she wanted to show the dog friendship on her own terms. *Pay no attention to the man in the barn. He'll wait.* But there was another whistle, a little different tone this time. Instantly the dog made her choice.

A cowboy-shaped silhouette appeared in the doorway. Jack braced his forearm on the barely open barn door and said a couple of indistinguishable words, his voice low and reassuring. The dog planted herself at his feet. Lily rose and followed the dog. Her inner independent woman groused at her every step of the way.

"You know better, girl."

Lily smiled. "Maybe, but I think I'll be okay."

"Talking to the dog. I know better than to whistle at a woman."

"Of course you do."

Jack folded his arms across his chest and took a wide stance, grinning. "You doubt me?"

"I know the difference between whistling *for* and whistling *at,* and I don't respond either way. But I can tell you know that." He backed into the barn as she approached, and she felt the summons in his eyes tugging at her female sensibility. "Thank you for helping Iris today. I'm a little embarrassed."

"About what?"

"Thirteen-year-olds, you know? Does your daughter talk back?"

"Not to me." He tucked his hands into the

pockets of his denim jacket. "But I don't get to see her that much."

"I have a feeling she wouldn't even if you did."

He lifted one shoulder. "I'm not her mother."

"Does she talk back to her mother?" He raised his brow, offering to let her off the hook. But no. "She doesn't, does she?" And he had to shake his head. "I read somewhere that teachers make the worst parents."

"I read that book, too, but I'm pretty sure it said *cowboys*." She laughed a little, and he smiled. "Feel better?"

"That *is* good medicine." She laid her hand on the cantle of a big Western saddle that was sitting on a homemade wooden saddle stand. A wooden stool and a tote box filled with familiar bottles and cans indicated that the saddle rated special care. She ran her hand over the smooth leather seat. "She's crushing on you big-time."

"She's what?"

"She has a crush on you. And you're her first, other than a couple of TV actors and the floppy-haired singer in some boy band. I was counting on that stage lasting a while longer."

He laughed. "Mike's been talking about getting a satellite dish ever since he heard you were coming. Would that help?"

"Maybe. It's confusing, being a girl that age. You take your teddy bear to bed at night, then wake up in the morning and stash some forbidden makeup in your backpack so you can put it on when you get to school."

"Is that what you did?"

"I guess." She swung her leg over the saddle, eliciting a leathery squeak as she took a seat. "For me it was horses. I noticed the horse first, and then maybe the rider. But mainly the horse."

"There you go. Like mother, like daughter."

"I hope not. I mean, I hope she doesn't…" She wrapped both hands around the saddle horn, tipped her head back and spoke to the rafters. "Just stick with the horses for a while, Iris." She smiled at Jack. "Good luck with that, huh?"

He lifted one shoulder. "Sounds like a plan to me."

"A good one. Iris's father was a cowboy."

He slid the stool between his legs and sat, eyes locked with hers. "What is he now?"

"Nothing. He no longer exists. It's hard to remember when he did."

"He's dead?"

"Who knows? He just…*isn't.*"

He pressed his lips together and gave a sympathetic nod. "Must be hard."

"Not at all. Iris is mine. Always has been. We've never needed—"

"I mean for Iris," he clarified quickly. "People like to know where they came from."

"She came from me. God planted a seed. That's what I was told when I asked." She gave a humorless chuckle. "Worked for me."

"You mad at me or something?"

"No. I'm not mad. Not at all." She studied him for a moment. He was everything she found appealing in a man. And everything she'd spent years avoiding. "Do you like being called a cowboy?"

"What's not to like?"

Typical nonanswer, she thought. "You're not a boy, for one thing."

"I'm not a cow, either. It's just a word."

"Well, he *was* a boy." She rarely said his name. Cody. She had no aversion to him. How could she? Without him, she wouldn't have Iris. Some women actually paid for sperm. He'd given it to her for nothing. She'd turned it into *everything*. "But a girl has a baby, she has to become a woman very quickly."

He took hold of the front pair of saddle strings and let them slide through his hand. "What did he say when you told him you were pregnant?"

"Nothing at first."

"Probably scared. What then?"

"He asked me how I knew it was his."

Jack shook his head. "Don't go there, boy. That is one stupid question."

"Did *you* go there?"

"Nope. We were both young, but I knew my wife better than I knew myself."

"Then why are you taking his side?" she asked indignantly.

"He has a side?"

"Cowboys stick together, is that the deal?"

"I'm gonna let you in on a little secret." He pushed the brim of his hat back and leaned closer. "There is no deal. No gentlemen's agreement. No brotherhood of the saddle tramps."

She smiled. "You ride alone?"

"Head held high, tall in the saddle." He lifted one shoulder. "If it helps any, he's the only one missin' out, no matter what he's doing now. I know that for a fact."

"Which you learned the hard way?"

"Better than *no* way." He touched her hand. "I don't know a whole lot about your situation, but I know something about your father. He's glad to have you here. Perked him right up when you told him you were coming to stay awhile."

"I didn't *tell* him. I asked. I do know how to pull my weight around here, and Iris will learn. It's a busy time of year. I know we can be useful. I only lost my job because of budget cuts. Last hired, first fired. Except I wasn't *fired*. He doesn't think I got fired, does he?"

"He thinks you were goin' along real good

until some idiot dug a damn barrow pit in the middle of your personal road and you got stuck."

She laughed. How long had it been since she'd heard a ditch called a *barrow pit?* "And he thinks he's towing me out?"

"Hell, no. You got yourself out, you and Iris. And you rode away, head held high, tall in the saddle."

"He didn't say anything like that."

"You asked me what he *thought*."

"My father's mind was never hard to read, but your interpretation sounds like a stretch." She glanced away. "Has he ever told you why I left the way I did?"

"He said he drove you away."

"No details?"

"I didn't need any. I was drivin' through life at least half drunk most of the time when I met Mike. High as a kite in Lowdown." He gave a dry chuckle, and she had to smile. "When drinking gets the best of a man, his family gets his worst."

"Such a deal," she said with a sigh.

"I've been sober almost six years. It's been longer than that for Mike." He looked puzzled. "You didn't know he'd quit drinking?"

"It's not something he's ever...*would* ever... actually..." She shrugged. "How would I know?"

"Damn. It wasn't my place to say."

"I'm glad you did. It's a relief. I dreaded having

Iris see him that way. He was never really mean, but he was hard. Just a very hard man."

"He works hard."

"Oh, yes, I'll give him that."

And then some. She'd stopped blaming him for the way he worked, the way he expected everyone else to toe the line he'd drawn for himself. And it wasn't just work. It was every aspect of a person's behavior—of *her* behavior, since the other person in the household had walked out with no thought of taking her daughter with her. Which, Lily had later come to understand, was for the better.

"What made him stop drinking?" she asked.

"You'll have to ask him. One thing I will say…" Jack nodded. "He helped me. Kinda the father I never had."

She laughed. "That makes two of us."

"You have him now. That's what counts, isn't it? That's all we have. Can't go back, and you wouldn't want to skip ahead."

"I guess." She glanced up at the brim of his black hat and smiled. "You're pretty smart for a cowboy."

"I only heard the first part of that."

He cupped her face in his warm hand, cosseting her chin in the smooth well of his palm, roughened fingers abrading her cheeks so gently she quivered inside. Heated gaze locked on hers, he leaned down slowly until breath as warm as a wish touched her skin. She tried to outlast his gaze, but expectation weighed heavily on her eyelids as his lips met hers, softly at first, a tender greeting. The words in her head dissolved into wonder.

She turned to him fully, found a handful of denim to hang on to and parted her lips for him.

And together they created the kiss they craved.

Chapter Four

The first calf came on a cold, clear morning when Jack was on hand to watch. The big black baldy cow lowered her hips, flanks undulating deeply as her muscles did their amazing work, pushing forth a big, watery bubble of life. Two small hooves, a nose, a head, and soon, *whoops!* Baby on the ground. It was a beautiful sight, a smooth, nearly silent process when everything fell into place the way nature intended. All a man had to do was sit quietly in the saddle, stand clear and appreciate the wonder. The mother moved quickly to clean her newborn while three mothers-to-be lumbered on over to investigate. Jack was the only male around, and he wasn't needed.

Maybe that was how true cowboys came up with their unassuming nature. Times like this, the cows did all the work. They could be mulish at times, and dumb, and even dangerous, but the bad bovine mother was a rarity—a humbling fact that hit home daily with a working cowboy. He was almost grateful when a little something went wrong and he had his chance to help make it right.

Jack had missed out on the births of his own two children. He'd hung out in the clinic lobby until a nurse had come to tell him he had a daughter. The second time around he'd waited a little while—an hour maybe—before heading over to Tommy Fisher's place to rope a few calves and chug a few cans of the local brew. Moose Drool wasn't his preferred brand, but it was what Tommy had in the cooler, and Jack had been chugging long past choosy when he'd wandered back over to the clinic to discover that his baby son and exhausted wife were both asleep. Two-year-old Becky wasn't interested in seeing him, either, or so his sister-in-law had told him when she ordered him to "go sleep it off."

Females were too damn touchy, he'd decided, and he'd proceeded to become someone unworthy of their touch. Becky didn't want to be around him half the time—the half when he was carrying a can of Drool around—and Edie finally decided the other half of his time wasn't worth the effort. The marriage and the fledgling ranch they'd started together were soon history.

But through it all, Jack had been a good hand. He'd worked for a couple of big ranches full-time before he'd gone out on his own as a day worker. He'd had to contend with a reputation for being "the best in the business when he's sober" until he'd met Mike Reardon. Mike offered plenty of work for a cowboy but no time for a drunk. The deal had saved Jack's life.

Mike's small operation hadn't required full-time help, but a couple of the members of his newly formed cattlemen's co-op needed seasonal help, and before long Jack had more work than he could keep up with. But Mike's jobs always came first. Jack never said as much, but his clients understood his commitment to Mike. Thanks to its founder—who had dodged the Big C bullet two years back—the co-op was growing. But lately nobody was talking about Mike's health. A friend was someone who let well enough alone, even when *not well enough* was beginning to show in a man's face. Life on the high plains was tough enough without asking questions prematurely.

But Jack knew. The fact that Mike wasn't supervising the unloading of the roofing materials was a sure sign he wasn't up to snuff this morning. Mike had promised to have the trucker unload the metal sheets onto the scaffold Jack had put up next to the barn. From the top of the hill overlooking the barn Jack could see that it wasn't happening. He nudged his mount into an easy lope.

When he got there, Jack helped the trucker and his sidekick transfer the roofing materials onto his scaffold, sent them on their way and headed for the house. He knew Iris was in school and Lily's car was nowhere to be seen, but Mike's pickup was parked outside, and Jack hadn't seen him around. He let himself in through the kitchen, hoping for coffee. There was none, which was surprisingly disappointing. He thought he'd un-loaded frivolous feelings like hope and disap-pointment from his baggage a long time ago.

Through the doorway to the front room he could see a pair of bare feet shelved above the floor on the extended footrest of Mike's favor-ite man-chair.

"The roofing materials just…" Jack stopped short in his tracks when he saw the man attached to the feet. His face was about the same color as the yellowing long-johns shirt topping the jeans his scrawny legs were swimming in. "What's goin' on?"

"Nothing. I'll be okay soon as I…" Mike dug his heels into the footrest and pressed down on the fake leather arms of the chair, but not much happened until Jack lent a hand. "You shouldn't be walking in the house without knocking. Give a holler, at least."

"I had them unload onto the scaffold I put up. I told Jensen not to count on me over to his place for the next couple of days."

"Why not?"

Why not? Hadn't Mike been the one to suggest he *snuff out the other end of the candle?*

Jack took a seat on the sofa. "I'm gonna get that roof fixed before—"

"You keep your promises, Jack. People know they can count on you. That's money in the bank."

"A hole in the roof is water in the barn." And the pain somewhere in Mike's body was written all over his face.

"I don't feel like laughin' right now."

"What *do* you feel like?"

"Felt like takin' a rest, but now that you've cut that short, I might as well get up on that roof and cover up them holes so your head stays dry." But he wasn't moving. "You ask me, that scaffold looks a little flimsy. You think it's gonna hold the roofing plus me and my tools?"

"I think it's gonna hold your corpse if you try gettin' on that roof. Built it sturdy enough to double as a funeral scaffold in case you keep going the way you have been." Jack reached across the arm of the sofa and tapped Mike's forearm with a loose fist. "Let the buzzards pick your damn bones clean."

"I hate buzzards." Mike let his head fall back against the generously padded chair. His skin sagged beneath his eyes and his cheekbones. "I want a coffin the color of the Montana sky. No flowers and no damn Indian wailing."

"I don't wail. As far as flowers go, you'll have at least two."

Mike looked stunned, as though he'd stepped into uncharted territory. "You think so?"

"Keeping your medical history a secret is one thing, but if you die, old man, they're gonna notice."

"I always figured I'd slip away quietly and let the lawyers handle the leavings."

"Leavings?" Jack shook his head in disgust, but then he brightened. "Hey. First calf dropped this morning. Black white-faced bull calf, slid out slick as a buttered noodle."

"Buttered noodle. You kids say the damnedest things." Mike's chuckle pumped some color into his cheeks. "This year's crop should all be black or black baldy. We'll qualify for certified Angus and certified grass-fed. That'll be my legacy."

"You go on with your legacy, man. I'm talkin' new life here."

"You didn't see any others? Did you take a head count? Anybody missing?" Jack's shake-nod-shake between questions seemed to go unregistered as Mike pulled himself to the edge of the seat. "I'll take a ride out there and have a look. I know those critters better than— Ah!"

"Your leg?"

"Damn, I'm getting old."

"Settle down," Jack insisted, but Mike was still trying to get unsettled. "I've got something to say." Mike froze, stared and finally nodded. "If you're not gonna let me do my job, I'll leave. I ain't hurtin' for work. Your daughter's here now, and your granddaughter. Maybe you've got enough—"

"You made your point." Mike's shoulders dropped, and then came his deep sigh. "They just got here. Finally. I don't care what brought them here, how desperate she had to be. They're here, and I need some time."

"Then you've gotta take care of yourself."

"I need to take care of my cows. If I can't get out there and see for myself…"

"What's it gonna be, Mike? I've always done it your way. You tell me what you want done, and I do it."

"Better than any man I know." The old man indulged Jack with a wistful smile. "Including me."

"I checked the cows an hour ago, moved a couple more in close. Not too many heavies yet, and I know the way you like to separate 'em out. You got a schedule in mind, I'll follow it. But if you start following *me* around after all the years I've worked here, pretty soon I'll be looking over my shoulder. And that ain't my style."

"Talkin' my ear off ain't your style, either, and it's not real good for my health."

"You got some kind of pain medication?"

"Why do you think I'm sleeping in the middle of the morning?"

"You get some rest, we'll take a pickup out there later."

Mike chuckled. "That ain't your style *or* mine."

"But the truth is, we're the only ones who'll know the difference." Jack glanced toward the hallway. "Is, uh…Lily around?"

"Ha!" Mike slapped his knee. "The only ones, huh?"

"She offered to help with, uh…a couple of chores she had in mind."

"She got a call from the school this morning," Mike said.

"Already? Iris still struggling with the language barrier?"

"She didn't say. Surprised she told me where she was going."

Jack lifted one shoulder. "You might try to do something about that particular barrier, Mike."

"From one father to another?"

"You got me there." Jack clapped his hat on,

started to leave and then turned. *Why the hell not?* "From somebody who likes your daughter."

There were two more calves by late morning, and three cows restlessly pacing, lying down, heaving themselves back up and moving on as though they were trying out mattresses in a furniture store. Jack had a keen eye, and as long as he wasn't spotting trouble he gave the natural process due respect and the cows their space. His boss was the same way, even if Mike liked to worry a little more than Jack did. Understandable, Jack allowed. Mike considered the cows his "bosses."

And Lily was Mike's daughter. Ever since Jack had come to work at the Rocking R he'd listened to Mike talk about the woman as though she was always busy doing good things, living an interesting life and letting him know the details, calling him back if she wasn't there to pick up the phone when he dialed her number.

As was his habit, Jack had taken him at his word. He knew what it was like to be a father whose mistakes had created the distance between himself and his kids, and he wanted to believe Mike still had a daughter. Why he seldom saw her, why she never came home for a holiday or took it upon herself to find out about her father's failing health, those were questions Jack didn't ask. He took Mike at his word, which was the extent of Jack's business. The job required all kinds of information with a daily dash of new details. As for the personal stuff, a little went a long way. Generally speaking.

Jack decided to get started on the barn and do as much as he could before the calf rush hit. From the roof he could see a good part of the pasture where he'd moved the heavies and where the excitement would soon take place. As long as he kept moving, the cold wind didn't bother him too much. Up and down the roof he went, checking the pasture on the climb and the highway on the slide. When Lily came back she would come see what he was doing and no doubt offer to help. He thought he would give her the good gloves, then looked at his hands and thought about the way her hand had felt on his cheek, its small size and feather weight, and he decided neither his good gloves nor his old ones would serve her.

Forget the roof. He would tell her that he needed her to go check cows.

No, he would tell her that *they* needed to go check cows.

Hell, he'd just checked the cows.

The rubber soles of his work boots ground grit loose from the old shingles as he sidestepped his way down the steep slope of roof, but he was one sure-footed Indian. He glanced up the highway. A semi and two pickups. No little red Chevy.

He reached over the edge of the roof and hauled up a sheet of roofing. He was finishing up a job that was half-done, which meant covering the old shingles with new metal. He might have done the job differently from the start—used slat board instead of screwing the steel down directly over the shingles—but he could make it work. He'd laughed when he'd watched a TV show with Becky the last time he'd visited the kids and some clothes designer kept saying, "Make it work." Jack had said to his daughter, "I don't know about you, but that guy could've been a cowboy." And she'd come back with, "He probably wanted to have some money in the bank."

The funny thing was, Jack did have some money in the bank. He hadn't always, but he did now. He hadn't pressed the issue, because he liked the way Becky was learning to make clothes so she could be on the show someday. She was a creative kid. Give her a problem, she would solve it with whatever she could find close at hand. Becky and Iris would hit it off right away.

If they ever got to meet.

Which wasn't likely.

The next time Jack sidestepped his way down the roof, he saw the red car turn off the blacktop and onto the gravel at the Rocking R sign. He was on his way down anyway, right? He made his way from the roof to the scaffold with a smile on his face before he realized he was taking away half the fun. *She* was supposed to come looking for *him*.

Hell, he wasn't into games. He lifted a pail full of screws onto the scaffold and looked around for anything else he might be needing soon, taking his time. Doing his own thing.

They met in the middle. Lily had gotten out of the car and she was heading for the barn. Jack was ambling toward the house.

"I thought somebody had put up a weather vane. Was that you?"

"Ain't that damn skinny."

"You had your arms out." She extended hers straight out from her shoulders and spun around, little-girl-like.

He laughed as he glanced at the car. "I was sliding a little. Where's Iris?"

"Taking the bus home, which is a good sign. You think she wants to ride with her mother when she's trying to fit in?"

"I'd take a ride in a car over that endless bus trip any day."

"Maybe in a few weeks, but right now I think she's busy making friends. Amazing, right? She didn't want any new friends. Didn't *need* any new friends."

"Who does? They get in the way. Always trying to get you to do stuff." He raised an eyebrow. "You wanna go for a ride? We got a few calves on the ground today."

She perked up real pretty. "I'll get my boots on."

"And check on Mike, would you?" She gave him a funny look, and he shrugged. "He wasn't feeling too good this morning."

"He looked okay when I left. What's he doing?"

"I was just about to check." It was one of those small lies known for whatever reason as *white*.

"Be my guest," she said, guardedly. He wasn't sure what she was guarding.

So he gave her a wink and a smile. "If it's all the same to you, I'll be the hired hand."

She turned away. "Here comes the bus. Maybe Iris should go with you. I should get something together for supper if Dad's..." She lifted a finger. "I'll be right back out."

"No rush. There's plenty of daylight left."

"Wave at the kids on the bus. You'll get her some points."

The oven door gave its opening squeak. Lily heard a pot lid rattle, but she waited for the closing squeak before entering the kitchen. Her father had already settled his skinny frame on the tall chair with the pullout steps that had been her seat at the kitchen table until she was about six. They had been three for supper in those days, but the pall over the table had been heavy by then, even for a six-year-old. Somehow she'd known—or feared—that Mama's presence was temporary, because it weighed the most.

"Are you all right?"

"Might've caught a bug or something." He raked his fingers through his full head of white hair. "Did you do some teaching today?"

"I subbed for the sub. The English teacher went to a workshop, and the sub called in at the last minute, said she couldn't make it. I think I earned myself some team-player credit with the principal. How 'bout you? Are you taking anything?"

"A little guff from my hired man. Why? What did he tell you?"

His agitation gave Lily pause. "What *should* he have told me?"

"Nothing. I'm okay. I may be gettin' there fast, but I'm not ready to be treated like an old man yet." He nodded toward the stove. "I'm making pot roast."

"Smells good. And you're not…" She gave a tight smile. "…not that old."

"I've still got things to do." He rose stiffly from the stool. "Calving started this morning, and I ain't been out there yet."

"You trust Jack, don't you?"

"Almost as much as I trust myself." He rubbed his left thigh. "Except for this damn leg. Feels like there's one bone in there that's a little older than the rest."

No surprise there. Ranching was hard physical work, and he'd been doing it all his life. He didn't need to do any riding with a bum leg. The urge to reach out to him confused her. She took a step back. "I'm gonna grab my boots and go check cows. Maybe you should take some ibuprofen or something, Dad. Iris can help you with supper."

He looked amused. It wasn't an expression she'd seen on him often.

"While you jump on a horse and take off riding? That's not gonna go over too good."

"When did you start caring which chores go over well? They all have to be done, right?" She gave a quick wave of her hand. "No, I'm not complaining. You were right. It's an important lesson, especially when times get tough. Besides, I need to get her some boots before she does too much more riding."

"Let me do that."

"No, I'll get them." She smiled. "I got a paycheck today."

The door to the mudroom banged, and Iris burst into the kitchen.

"Hey, Mom, Jack's waiting for you!" She dropped her books on the tiny kitchen table. "Can I go, too?"

"Not this time. I'd like you to set the table and help Grandpa with…" She turned to find her father bracing a hand on the back of the kitchen stool. "Are you sure you're okay, Dad?"

He waved his free hand. "Just get goin', girl. I'm just hungry is all. My stomach's gonna start suckin' the marrow outta my backbone pretty soon."

"Eww." Iris made a horrified face.

"Eww is right. Don't wait for us. You two go ahead and eat."

The horses had spring in their step, and she thought it was as much the season as the stride. The air was crisp, but it carried a promise. Sun and moisture were all the land needed, in that order. Newborns did better in rain than in snow. But Lily's mount cared only that the air was infused with the promise of change, and the sense of it had the horse prancing.

"Did I tell you?" she asked, then realized she hadn't told him anything. They'd saddled up and headed out. He had a way of not asking that allowed time for thought. "Dad was making supper."

"Guess he's doing okay, then."

"Other than complaining about aging limbs, which I guess…" She shrugged. "Has to be normal, right? The *new* normal? Dad's old normal was supper at five, followed by chores. Unless he threatened to do your chores himself, which meant supper could wait." But maybe not for Dad these days. He looked like he needed to eat. Or something. "He made pot roast."

Jack seemed intent on the cows, but his smile said she had his ear. "He swears by your recipe."

"Recipe?" She laughed. "There's no recipe."

"I've seen it. It's on a card with a bunch of others in a box that says *Lily's Recipe Box* on top."

"Oh." Now that he mentioned it, she remembered the box. She smiled again, remembering the fifteen-year-old who'd decorated it and filled it with recipes collected on index cards. "I was going to take that with me when I got married. Not when I graduated from high school and went to college, but later, after I graduated from college, taught school for two years and then got married. That was my plan."

"And your boyfriend's plan?"

"Who knows? We didn't talk much. It wasn't exactly you tell me yours and I'll tell you mine."

He glanced at her, surprised, then shrugged and turned back to surveying the herd. "How was school today? Kids pretty rowdy?"

"Nobody gets rowdy in my class. I run a tight ship, even when I'm only teacher for a day. I might look fragile, but I'm one tough flower."

"Looks don't say much for a person, and even

if they did, *fragile* isn't the word your looks say to me. *Tough* wouldn't be it, either."

"What, then?"

"Strong heart. One of my grandmas, the oldest one—you know, Indians have a lot of grandmas—she was a big woman. She could hold three little cousins on her lap and one under each arm. Doctors used to tell her if she got any bigger she'd have a heart attack. She lived to be ninety-seven." He glanced at her. "Strong heart."

"You're saying I'm beginning to look fat?"

"The opposite. I'm saying it wouldn't kill you to eat more."

"Good to know."

"That's not all I see when I look at you, but it's all I'm ready to admit to," he said, and she warmed to his smile.

"I'm sure your grandmother was a wonderful person, but I have to say, that's the most unusual compliment anyone's ever paid me." She gave a mock scowl. "It *was* a compliment, wasn't it?"

"Absolutely," he said absently as his attention skipped past her.

He nodded toward a scrawny ponderosa pine and urged his horse ahead. Lily followed suit, distracted from his discovery by the beauty of the way he swung down from the saddle in one lithe, fluid motion. He squatted on his heels in the tall grass. She rode up beside him and started to dismount.

"I got this." He stood as smoothly as he'd dismounted, arms full of slimy black calf. "Little one needs help, and Bunny's our best baby carrier. How 'bout you?"

"We already know I ride small in the saddle." She was already tucking it under and sucking it in, creating a hollow between her belly and the saddle horn. "But not quite as small as the last time I did this," she noted as he draped the squirmy calf over her belly and thighs.

"Perfect," he said. "You were made for calf carrying. Little heifer. Can't be more than an hour old."

"What about the mom?"

"I'll find her and come back for her." He looked up at her. "All the supplies are in the tack room. You remember how to bottle feed? 'Cause that ain't my job."

"Dad used to say it was a woman's job."

"Which stands to reason, right? Anything to do with milk, a man's all thumbs."

"Really?" She secured her grip on the frightened calf's hind legs while Jack mounted up again. When he was settled, she smiled. "What do you do with all those thumbs if there's no woman around?"

"We call it cowboy ingenuity." He glanced into

the shallow draw below, another scrub pine, a lone cow. "I'll run her in. She looks okay, but maybe she's got a little mastitis. Or a bad case of meanness. You never know."

Back at the barn Jack lifted the calf from Lily's lap, nestled it in a pile of straw and then put Bunny in a stall. Within minutes Lily heard him ride away. She rubbed the calf down, trimmed the umbilical cord and dabbed it with an iodine solution, found the colostrum replacement, a couple of calf bottles that needed washing—men!—and a package of new nipples. Then she headed for the house.

Lily took a quick glance as she passed the dining room. Iris was just sitting down to eat with her grandfather. "Sorry," Mike called out. "We couldn't wait any longer. Everything okay?"

"Damn cow won't take her calf." Lily stuck her head in the doorway. "I mean, the dam won't take her calf."

"We've got an orphan already?" Mike slid his chair back from the table.

"You two finish eating. Jack and I can take care of this. He's bringing the cow in."

"I wanna see," Iris said, scraping her chair across the wood floor.

"Don't worry," Mike said, and there was more chair wrangling. "If we can't get the cow to take her baby, you'll be seeing a lot of that calf. And the damned dam will be goin' down the road."

The threat of banishment was not what Lily needed to hear. Without another word she prepared warm colostrum replacement in a clean calf-feeding bottle and left the house. She'd left the little heifer wrapped in an old wool blanket in the straw nest Jack had made, but she found her uncovered and shivering. The good news was that she was standing on all fours. Maybe Lily didn't look so tough, but in her eyes the little calf sure did. She didn't know quite what to do with the rubber nipple at first, so Lily rocked the bottle in the calf's mouth and squeezed rhythmically, and soon she had the baby sucking for dear life. Literally.

Lily smiled. "You'll be fine," she said softly. "Your mama's just a dumb ol' cow. She doesn't know how beautiful you are. When Jack brings her in, she'll get a chance to change her mind. One chance. If she still doesn't get it, don't worry. I get it. Iris gets it."

"Jack gets it."

Startled, Lily tried to cover with a laugh. "Jack walks on cat's paws."

"The horse he rode in on doesn't, and neither does that mad cow we were chasing." He squatted on his heels beside her, pulled one leather glove off and touched the sticky tuft of black hair on top of the calf's head. The glove he'd dropped into the straw held the shape of his fingers.

"Did you get her in?"

"Yeah, but you can bet come next Tuesday she'll be bound for the sale barn."

"Unless she takes her baby."

"Not a chance." He made a teasing attempt to dislodge the nipple, but the calf hung on. Jack chuckled. "Baby's doing just fine where she is."

"Mothering is a strong instinct. There's always a chance."

"That's what I said about this same bovine bitch last year. She finally took her calf, but she was none too willing." He snapped up his glove and slapped it across his chaps-clad knee. "It's too bad. She produces a nice calf to start with."

"Should we try? We've got her suckling."

"*You've* got her suckling. That's not my job."

"Cowboys," she said disgustedly, and then, *"Men."*

"Guilty on both counts." Jack pushed himself up, hands against his knees. "Here come the boss and his new sidekick."

Lily looked up as her father and daughter walked into the barn. Iris was wearing the blue-and-white toque Lily had knitted for her, braided yarn dangling from the earflaps. She'd stopped wearing it when Lily had told her they were moving. Lily smiled.

"He calls the cows bosses," Iris said as she jerked her thumb over her shoulder toward the man limping behind her. Her blue eyes brightened at the sight of the nursing calf. "Awww."

"Guess that makes him the boss of all bosses," Jack said. "Right, Mike?"

"Right. We'll take over now. You two go eat."

While the three adults looked on, Iris took bottle and calf in hand as though she'd been handling them for years. She wore a kid's love-at-first-sight look. Lily glanced at the men, who had warm heart written all over their hard-edged faces.

Her father suddenly came to his senses. "Food's no good cold."

Jack questioned him with a look, but the comment was déjà vu for Lily. Anything else could go cold, but not Dad's food.

With supper cleared, youngster tucked in and oldster retired to watch TV, Jack tortured himself a little, lingering at the back door, letting Lily delay him with a few words about nothing much, and then a few more. She asked about feeding time for the calf even though she knew the answer better than he did. He ran his fingertips down her sleeve as he asked about her plans for tomorrow. She tipped her head to one side, straightening his jacket collar as she asked about his, and he took his time replying, hoping to draw out the moment.

"Do you always get up that early?" she asked. He nodded.

"Do you ever take a day off?"

"Try to. Depends."

"On what?"

"The cows. The boy always depends on the cows." She questioned him with a look, and he gave a lopsided smile. "The cowboy. That's what you like about me."

"Who said I like anything about you?"

Her eyes said. He kept right on smiling.

"But the man has other considerations, like the season, the weather, my employers, my kids. I go up north to see my kids whenever I can. Whenever their mother gives me the high sign, I head up to the Hi-line," he said, referring to the part of the state north of Highway 2.

"How often does that happen?"

He lifted one shoulder. "Not often enough."

"Do you take your trailer?"

"Try not to. Damn spendy pullin' that thing around. If your dad wasn't lettin' me park it here I'd trade it for something smaller."

"So it's...comfortable?"

"You wanna check it out?" He let the invitation shine from his eyes a little bit, but not too long. No pressure. "Tomorrow, maybe. Give you the thirty-second tour."

"I'm just curious."

"I'm angling for attracted, but I'll take curious."

He touched her cheek with the only part of him that was clean enough—he'd washed his hands for supper—and smiled as her eyes drifted closed. He traced a path along her cheekbone with his forefinger, touching the point of her chin with his thumb. He threaded his fingers through her hair and lowered his head as she lifted her hands to his waist, and he covered her mouth with slow, sensual kisses. Finally he whispered against her moist lips, "It's a start."

Chapter Five

Lily was more than curious, and she was definitely, deeply, attracted. And reckless and silly, so girlishly silly to be sneaking out of her father's house at some obscure wee hour in the morning. But she'd lain awake long enough with the taste of Jack's kiss on her lips. Through the mist made by her breath in the pure, cold air she set her sights on the light in the window of his trailer. He was no slacker, this cowboy. If he asked, she could help with the cows. If he was already out, she would wait.

Hula met her outside the door, whined a little, wagged a lot. The light went out just as Lily readied her knuckles, but the door swung open before she touched it.

"I thought you might need—"

He plucked her off the ground, swept her into his arms as if she weighed nothing and found her mouth unerringly with his. He was warm and damp and—she soon discovered—completely naked. His skin smelled of sandalwood soap, and his mouth tasted of peppermint. She helped him take off her coat and raised her arms so he could peel off her sweater, but when she tried to undo her jeans, he stilled her hand, lifted her onto the loft bed and pulled the boots off her feet. Then he did all the unbuttoning, and she lay back to let him strip her of her jeans. Then, finally, he joined her in his bed.

His first kisses were gently persuasive—warm, moist touches that left her skin tingling and her mind racing with thoughts she wished would go away. She wanted this, and she *wanted* to want this. She reached for him, arms around his back, taking the measure of its contours, the way it tapered from strapping shoulders to slender waist, the feel of a body honed by a man's work. A welcome image traveled from her hands to her brain. No words. Just pictures of Jack's strong back and his powerful arms doing the heavy lifting his job demanded. Watching him in her mind and feeling him under her hands was intoxicating. She wanted more.

She took his gentle approach to heart and answered with all the pressure and heat and hunger she felt, and he replied with an urgent kiss. He'd come to the table courteously, keeping his hunger in check, but her signal was unmistakable. She'd come to him willingly. Everything on the table was his for the taking. His breath warmed the deep well of her ear, while her lobe got a nipping. Feathery kisses made her neck tingle, and the sensation spread like ripples in water.

Her breasts responded instantly when he turned his attention to them. He slipped one bra strap off her shoulder, and she took a slow, deep breath, filling herself with his spicy scent, relishing the wonder of wanting, the pleasure of feeling his every touch throughout her body. He knew where she wanted most to be caressed, and his approach was deliberately, maddeningly measured. When he touched her nipple, her breath wobbled. Quickly he covered her mouth with his, as though he'd caught her drowning. She tried to reach the back of her bra, but he beat her to it, and the band went slack, freeing her to want more.

He suckled one nipple while he abraded the other with deft fingers and calloused palm. His long, hard penis was cosseted between his stomach and her hip, and when he rocked it a bit she shifted her hips, wordlessly offering the perfect cradle. He pressed but did not pursue. Not yet. She held herself back, containing her pleasure until it took over and voiced itself. Was that her? It sounded like a small creature in pain.

His fingers played her the length of her torso, and when they reached her panties, he shifted to her side and stroked her over the damp, silky fabric before tucking his hand inside and petting her tenderly, his fingertips approaching, then maddeningly retreating, only to approach again. At last they parted her protective flesh and slid over the slickness of her private flesh until she cried shamelessly for him. He kissed her mouth, his tongue mimicking the movement of his finger, reaching down to lift her up and up, until she quaked and shuddered beneath his ministrations. She slid her hand between them, reaching for his penis, but he kept it locked down tight despite his own growing demands.

"I don't suppose you brought a condom," he whispered.

She groaned. "I didn't think..."

"No worries." With a low chuckle he kissed her temple. "Don't start thinking now. I've got us covered."

If she'd been thinking, the moment it took him would have been made sweet by the notion that he didn't keep condoms beside his bed. But she hadn't thought, and she wasn't thinking, and his absence left her wanting him. She was all about wanting him.

He returned quickly. She was waiting and wanting, but not watching. He pulled the blankets over himself and covered her with his body. She was ready, but he made her more ready until she clutched his rock-hard buttocks and drew him inside her. Wet as she was, she still felt a pinch, and she gasped. He tried to withdraw. But she dug her nails into his solid flesh and it was his turn to groan.

"Don't stop," she pleaded.

"Don't let me hurt you."

"I've got you where I want you," she whispered. "You can't hurt me."

"Tell me if I do." He filled her slowly. "I want to do right by you."

"I don't know what that means."

"It means we do it together," he said, pouring the words into her ear as he touched her center with his tip.

And then she was on her way to the stars.

Jack adjusted the blankets over Lily's shoulder, bundling them together so tightly he could feel a tremor run through her. "Are you cold?"

"Oh, no." She snuggled against his chest. "But it's cold outside. Feels like snow."

"Yeah, it's comin' right along with the calves. I pulled one already tonight. I was just getting cleaned up when you..." He slid his fingers into her silky hair. He could feel the calluses on his palm catch it like a rough fingernail. It was his right hand, his roping hand. His caressing hand. He felt big and bristly and unsuitable for this small, soft woman, but he had no intention of stepping aside for a softer, smoother man—or, for that matter, for *any* man. "Did you know I was thinking about you?" he whispered.

"How would I know that?"

"No idea. I'm just a man." He meant to be flip, but it didn't come off that way. "I opened the door, and there you were, and I thought, God, the woman is a mind reader."

"I knew you'd be checking cows during the night. I thought I could help." She paused. "Does that sound plausible?"

"Absolutely."

"I believed it."

"You turn that thought into an offer to pull the next calf, and I'll take you up on it. Let's see your arm." He drew it from the blankets and stretched it at an angle to avoid the low ceiling. "I don't think your reach is long enough."

"And yours is?"

"Everywhere that counts." She groaned, and he laughed. "Yeah, you should know."

"I should, shouldn't I?"

Her laughter picked up a few long seconds after his left off. He growled and play-bit her shoulder.

"But I wasn't there for the big moment. What was the outcome?"

"Liar." He tucked her arm back under the covers and drew her hand down between their bellies.

"Not that moment." She laughed again. "The *calf.*"

"Little bull calf had both front feet back. Once I had 'em pulled forward, mama did the rest, but she sure didn't want any part of me."

"Don't take it personally. Male is as male does. Did you have to use the calf puller?"

"Just the chain." He flattened her hand on his belly and dragged it over his torso until he could press it to his chest. He couldn't bring himself to say what he wanted to say, *touch my nipples,* but he wanted her to feel his heart beating. "Let's go back to the part where I opened the door and there you were," he said softly. "My God, there you were."

"You knew it was me."

"I had a real strong feeling." He rubbed her hand over him, caused a catch in his breath when her little fingernail ticked his nipple. "Yeah, I knew. The way I was feeling, it couldn't have been anybody else."

"I wasn't expecting this. Not at all. This isn't the way I...do things."

"It isn't?" He lifted her hand to his mouth and kissed her fingertips. "Do we need any special equipment for doing things your way? Show me what you got, woman."

"What I've got—usually—is good sense. I'm careful. I'm not—"

"I used a condom. That's my special equipment. Nothing fancy, but sturdy. Like me."

Through the narrow window the moon lit her smile. "I wasn't prepared for you, and I should have been. You were all I could think about from the moment you left the house." She tucked her chin and leaned closer so that he felt her warm breath on his neck when she confided, "This isn't me. I don't know who this person is who's feeling so good to be inside this body."

"A few minutes ago that was me," he reminded her, stopping just short of adding, *And don't you ever forget it.* "I don't know who's in there now."

"A happy woman. Inside and out, every bit of me feels content."

He touched her temple. "How 'bout in here?"

"Amazed. Is that a feeling? But I don't want you to think I came out here looking for sex. I was just..." She leaned back until the moon kissed her face again, brightening her eyes. "...looking for you."

"I'm glad you found me before I did something crazy." He rolled to his back and grinned at the ceiling. "Like breaking into the house to get to you." He really had thought about it. Not breaking in exactly, but… "A guy could get himself shot breaking into Mike Reardon's house in the middle of the night."

"And you thought it was his Irish roots he was putting down in the garden."

"That's how he grows such big honkin' tomatoes?"

She laughed. "My God, you're fun."

"You are, too. But don't go all bashful on me again, girl."

"Girl?"

"Woman." He groaned. "Go easy on me, Lily. I'm trippin' over my own tongue. I've never been with a teacher before."

She rose up on one elbow. "Put your tongue in my mouth again, cowboy. Let me teach you what I have in mind."

The sweetness of her kiss took a backseat to the feel of her breast brushing against his arm. He slid his fingers into her hair and enriched her kiss with a touch of tongue. "You're some kind of woman, Lily. The good kind," he whispered. His next kiss bore a touch of regret. "I have to go."

"I'll help you. But…" Her kiss backed up her appeal. "…one more minute."

"Another minute and I'll have to stay." His kiss was quick, hard and final. "Go to sleep."

But she followed his lead, sitting up beside him, throwing off the blankets as he did, then waiting, watching him. He had to duck. She didn't.

"I'm going with you." She found her sweater at the far side of the bed. "Was I wearing a bra?"

"A triple hooker." He dangled it by a strap. She thanked him, and he followed up with her bikini panties. "You were wearing these, too. Least I'm pretty sure they're yours." He held them up to the light. "Look like your size. Were they white?"

She snatched them from his hand. "Are you a collector?"

"Victoria isn't the only one who has a secret. I like the seven-day set. Keeps me organized."

"Right."

"You've shown me yours, but I've never shown you mine."

"I'm guessing you don't have any," she said, as she lifted her butt off the mattress to pull hers into place. "You're the commando type," she said as she slipped her bra straps over her shoulders.

"I try real hard to defy stereotyping." He reached behind her and fastened the hooks. "I'll let you find out for yourself when we get to know each other better."

* * *

She was pulling her sweater over her head as he slid off the bed. The bench below the loft was cold underfoot. The linoleum floor was even colder. This was no place to bed a woman you wanted to impress, he thought as he stepped into his jeans.

"You should go back to the house and get some sleep," he told her. "I could use your help tomorrow. I need to get over to the Jensen place for a few hours."

"Could you toss my jeans up here?"

He pulled his thermal shirt over his head. "I'll walk you home if you want."

The first thing he saw when his head popped through the neck of his shirt was her bare leg dangling over the edge of the bed. The other leg slid down beside it.

"There they are." She pointed to the far side of the compact kitchen. "Right where you threw them. It would be so much easier if you'd just hand them to me. I'm going with you. I came dressed for the job. Really, that was why…at least, I thought that was why I came."

"Your intentions were pure and honorable." He handed up her jeans. "I don't doubt that. Did you bring gloves?"

"In my pockets."

"Hat?"

"Okay, you got me. No hat. I must be in heat."

"Good. You can keep me warm."

When they got to the barn Rusty was waiting to go out again. Once the calves started dropping, a good cow pony knew what was required of him as well as the cowboy who rode him.

"We'll ride double," Jack said. "I'll be your windbreak."

"That sounds gallant," Lily said. "Romantic, even."

He chuckled as he seated the split-ear bridle. *Romantic* was good. He wasn't so sure about gallant. No way was he going after another horse tonight. He turned to offer her a leg up, but she was a step ahead of him, boosting herself aboard.

"Bareback?" Watching her swing her leg over Rusty's rump, he couldn't help remembering her lovely bare ass.

"Oh, yes." She smiled down at him. She clearly knew how nice and nimble she looked climbing aboard the tall horse. Obviously her body hadn't lost its horse sense. "I'll have a windbreak and a hot seat."

He put his tool bag—two canvas sacks tied together—over the horse's withers and nodded for her to slide forward. "You're driving. We've got a tailwind headin' out."

They rode unhurriedly through the herd. Backlit by a full moon, the gathering clouds cast an eerie glow over the prairie and lent fluorescence to the bald faces of cows drifting silently like boats in a lake of grass. There was no sign of trouble. The newborn Jack had wrestled into the world earlier was nestled comfortably in the portable calving shelter. His mother had cleaned and nursed him, and now she, too, was resting. She still had no use for Jack, but she was too tired to care what he was doing in her territory as long as he posed no threat to her baby.

On the way back to the house Jack took pleasure in the feel of Lily's body resting against his back, her arms wrapped around his waist, her thighs tucked behind his. The cold wind in his face was no bother at all. He rode right up to the back door and softly, reluctantly told Rusty to *ho*.

"Oh." Lily peeled herself off his back. "I think I drifted off a little."

"If you can do that you're a better cowboy than I am."

"I only half drifted," she said. "I was there if you needed me. But all's quiet on the Western front, and I didn't even get to do anything. I'll go feed the calf."

"I'll take care of her. You've got your own youngster to look after. It'll be daylight soon."

"I did my part when I was Iris's age. A few responsibilities can't hurt. One step at a time, huh?"

"One step, one change, one day," he said, as he

turned and caught her, pulling her close before she could dismount. "One night," he whispered, as he touched his lips to hers.

The back door opened.

"Well, *there* you are."

Iris.

Jack took his time breaking off the kiss. He came up smiling, but only for Lily. She pushed against his chest, and he let her slide slowly to the ground.

"We were checking the cows," Lily said.

"Plain English, Mom." Standing on the steps with her flannel nightgown trailing below her jacket and over her jeans, Iris folded her arms over her chest. "I haven't mastered Montana slang yet. Cows aren't anything like Hooters, are they?"

Jack nearly choked.

"You can be sure Hutterites don't take any lip from their kids, slang or otherwise," Lily said. "And right now it's calving season twenty-four seven until the last calf is safely on the ground. And your job—"

"Is feeding the calf, which is what I was just about to do, but either I woke Grandpa up or…" Iris shook her head and cast Lily a worried look. "I think he's sick."

"What's wrong?"

Jack swung his leg over Rusty's head and slid to the ground. "Iris, take Rusty to the barn for me and put him in the big stall. Think you can take the bridle off?"

"Sure. And then I'll feed CC. For Cute Calf."

"GG." Jack handed Iris the reins. "Good girl."

"Can I ride him?"

Iris bunched her nightgown up, Jack gave her a leg up and off she went. Rain or shine, dark or dawn, Rusty knew his way to the barn.

"Do you know what's wrong?" Lily followed Jack into the house.

"Not yet." He turned to hold the door for her, and as she passed he added, "Keep your cool, okay?"

"What cool?"

Mike was slumped over the kitchen table, head nested in folded arms. Jack started toward him, but Lily had the advantage of being one step ahead.

"Dad? Are you...?" She leaned down and sniffed. "He's drunk."

"Drunk? No way. He's—"

"He reeks of whiskey." She took the resolute position her daughter had assumed when she'd caught them kissing, arms folded, shoulders squared. "He's too...too damn old for this. He said he'd quit."

"Nobody's ever too old. And he *has* quit." He laid his hand on Mike's shoulder and squeezed gently. "Mike, let's get you to bed."

"Jack?" Mike lifted his head and looked up to be sure. "Jack, I know you. I trust..." He shook his head. Jack saw the telltale wooziness in Mike's eyes, and he could feel the buzz along with the shame. "I gotta get out to my cows, Jack. Those bosses need me. I gotta...kill the pain, that's all. Real pain, you know? The kind you can't..." He tried to get up on his own, but he sat right back down again. "I can't go back to bed."

Jack lifted the old man's arm around his neck. "Yes, you can," he said as he hauled him to his feet.

"I got work to do, Jack."

"Not tonight. It's all done." He nodded at Lily, signaling her to step aside. She did, but she was hanging on to her folded arms. Or they were hanging on to her. "Hey, you know what? Lily helped me make the rounds. How do you like that?"

"That's good." Mike leaned heavily on him, and Jack wasn't sure whether it was the booze or his weak leg. "I like that, I do."

"We need to get you something for pain."

"I don't like that stuff, Jack. Don't trust pills. You buy a bottle, says *whiskey* on the label, you know what that means."

"Yeah, we know what that means. Is it helping?"

"Some. It's helping some."

* * *

Lily watched the two men round the corner and disappear into her father's bedroom. She could hear their voices, but she couldn't tell what they were saying. She waited, arms wrapped around herself, consciously holding herself together. This wasn't going to work. Her daughter shouldn't have had to see her grandfather in that condition.

"What's going on?" she asked Jack when he returned.

"You'll have to ask him."

"I'm asking *you*."

He glanced away and shook his head.

"He's drunk. That much I can see. Smell. Hear in his voice."

Jack nodded.

"Stop playing games, Jack. Just tell me."

"It's no game. You two have to talk to each other, Lily. It's not my place."

"The Rocking R might not be your place, but you treat it as though…as though you know it well and you love it."

He nodded.

"Well, my dad's a part of this place, and so am I, so why are you treating me like a stranger all of a sudden? A gate-crasher?" She scowled. "You crashed my gate a little while ago, and now you can't even talk to me?"

Jack tipped his head to one side as though he

wasn't sure he'd heard her correctly. "Crashed your gate? Those are some pretty scary words, woman."

"It's a metaphor. I was just being—"

"Clever." He shook his head. "It won't work with me, Lily. I don't know where I stand with you, but I know where I stand with me. And it sure as hell ain't between you and your father."

"Good to know," she said quietly, studying the toes of her boots.

"I'm no gate-crasher, and neither are you. Any chance of getting turned away, we walk. Right? Because it hurts to get turned away." He slipped his arm over her shoulders and tucked her under his arm. "But we keep the hurt to ourselves."

"We cowboy up," she said.

"Damn straight."

"So, my dad. Is he…?"

He touched two fingertips to her lips. "Don't ask me anymore. Ask *him*." She pressed her lips together and nodded stiffly. "What are you afraid of?" And then, gently, "Getting turned away?"

"That won't happen. If it does, well…"

Slam!

"She's ba-ack," Iris chirped, shedding her jacket. She stopped short and hiked one eyebrow. "Every time I open a door, there you are, in each other's face."

Jack laughed. "You have a way with words, just like your mother."

"I have my own way with words, and it's wickeder than hers. So you might wanna try not to look so guilty." She hung her jacket on a hook beside the door. "Is Grandpa okay?"

Lily laid warm hands on her daughter's cold cheeks. "We told him we—the three of us—were looking after everything, and he went to bed."

"So he's okay?"

"Tired," Jack said. "Calving season is the busiest time around here."

"I took care of Rusty and CC." Iris turned to her mother. "So you can't expect me to get up at the butt crack of dawn and go to school."

"Of course not. You're already up. And if I'm not mistaken, the sky will be mooning us any minute now."

Iris groaned.

"You're a ranch kid now," Jack said. "So let's you and me go crack some eggs, kid."

"I don't eat breakfast."

"Ranch kids eat breakfast." Jack pushed the café curtain aside and peeked through the window. "Uh-oh. Here comes trouble."

Chapter Six

The weather had been too good to hold. Gunmetal-gray clouds were never a good sign, but with the sudden drop in temperature, early spring reverted to late winter and heavy wet snow piled up quickly. School buses were turned back, and the highway that ran past the Rocking R was soon deserted.

Iris waved off Lily's suggestion that she go back to bed after breakfast and insisted that she wanted to help. By noon she'd checked cows with Jack while Lily took care of barn chores. Then she changed her wet clothes and gamely climbed back into the saddle for a second round, this time with Lily filling out the team. By suppertime Iris had witnessed four births, one calf pulling and one death, all for the first time. Together the three of them had run the mother of the dead calf back to the barn, where Jack introduced her to Iris's CC.

"She's going to hurt her," Iris said, lunging for her calf when the black cow kicked without connecting.

Lily grabbed Iris's shoulders and felt her trembling. "Jack won't let that happen. It takes a little time."

Iris stepped away from her mother, standing strong but clear of kicking range. "I can feed her."

"If this works, you won't have to." Squatting on his heels, Jack corralled the calf between his thighs and soothed it with his hands. "Don't worry, ranch kid, there will be more orphan calves in your future."

The cow had a heavy bag, and the calf had a hefty hunger. Jack waited for them both to calm down before manually priming a teat, but as soon as he tried to attach the calf, the cow kicked at it again.

"Oh! That's so mean." Iris was all over the calf once Jack had pulled it beyond kicking reach. The calf seemed grateful. Iris turned CC's face and her own up for Lily's scrutiny. "Her feelings are hurt, Mom. You can see it in her eyes."

"Ranch kids can't get too attached," Lily warned.

"How can you look at that face and not..."

Iris picked up the calf—an armful for a thirteen-year-old—and stood in front of the cow. "Look at this face. You can't turn this— Whoops!" The cow rattled her cross-tie chains. "She *can* turn this down."

"They go by smell." Jack was unbuckling the leg bands on a set of hobbles.

"Oh. Well, that's just dumb."

"She's a cow. They're pretty dumb by definition." Jack patted the cow's flank. She swung her head toward him and gave him a look. "Sorry, boss. The easy way ain't workin' for us. Gotta use the kickers."

"See?" Iris said to the cow. "You're just making it harder for yourself. You *are* dumb."

"Intelligence has nothing to do with it," Lily said. "Smell has an effect on women, too. That's a scientific fact."

Iris sniffed at Jack. "He smells like a horse, Mom."

Lily raised an eyebrow and offered a tight-lipped smile. Jack laughed.

"All right, you guys go by what*ever*. CC and I are going by who's gonna feed us." Back on the dirt floor with her calf, Iris stroked its silky black ear. "And we're hungry, aren't we, CC?"

"Me too. Stand back, ladies." Jack approached the cow from the side and ran his hand slowly down her leg. When he reached the right spot, he eased the nylon leg band into place and buckled it with the deft efficiency of a roper tying a piggin string, talking quietly all the while. "Lily, Iris and I can finish up here if you want to go back to the house and feed your starving workers."

"I'll whip up something quick." *And check on Dad.* But she wouldn't confront him, she told herself. It would be pointless.

Tending a pot on the stove, his back to the small alcove that served as a mudroom, Mike appeared steady on his feet. She used the boot-jack and hung her jacket on a hook. Her father turned his head when he heard her, nodded and kept right on stirring.

It was the same next-day silence she had known all too well when she was growing up. But she wasn't having it, not this time. She'd grown up. If this was just a temporary tumble off the wagon, time would tell. But if there was more to it...

"Aren't you going to say anything?" she asked quietly, immediately abandoning her plan not to confront him.

"I'm making some chili. Figured I'm not out there working, least I can do is cook up some chow." Slowly he placed the wooden spoon on a saucer and turned to face her. "I don't know what I can say, Lily."

"You can tell me what's going on."

"I took a drink." He glanced away, and she noticed the dark circles under his eyes. His face had aged noticeably in just one day. "It's been years. Hell, one day I just quit. More like I changed my mind, put the bottle back in the cupboard and said not today. Same thing the next day, and the next. Opened the cupboard, closed it up again. I guess I never used the word *quit*." He shook his gray head. "Yesterday I opened the cupboard and I took a drink. And then another, a short one, and then another one. I gotta say, it did help."

"Help what?"

"My leg's been bothering me a lot lately." As if to prove it, he used the edge of the counter as support as he made his way over to the kitchen stool.

"I know you don't like doctors, Dad, but—"

"Oh, hell, I love doctors." He winced as he took a seat. "I've been seeing this one—she's a real peach."

"Seeing?"

"Professionally. She's too young for me." He gave a dry chuckle. "Story of my life, I guess. But this one looks after me pretty good, health-wise. She wants me to get some tests, and I told her I'd do it as soon as we're done calving."

"She must have some idea what's causing the pain."

"I'm gettin' old, girl. I've been working hard

all my life. You gotta give me that. I started out there this morning, and that cold wind blew me right back inside. It's like Jack says. I've gotta start letting people help me. He's been with me a long time, and I know by now I can trust him. He's a good man, Lily. Good man." He stared at her for a moment as though if he looked hard enough he could tell whether she agreed. Finally he shrugged. "But I hate this. I just wanna be out there myself. Watching those bosses work for me, dropping some of the finest calves you'll find anywhere—it don't get any better."

Lily sighed. That had been maybe the most words he'd ever strung together for her in the shortest time, and the answer to her question still hadn't been among them.

"What did the doctor say about waiting to get the tests done?"

"She said it's up to me. Which it is."

"Okay. I won't worry about it, then."

"That's good," he said as she turned on her heel. "You've got enough to—"

She faced him again, her socks turning the move into a pirouette. "Dad, why do you trust Jack and not me? Because he's never disappointed you?"

"Jack works for me. I pay him to do a job, and he's never let me down." He nodded once. "You're my daughter. It's up to me not to let *you* down."

"Then tell me what's going on with you."

"You've been gone a long time. There's been…"

He gave her that look again, sizing her up. She wasn't Jack. She wasn't a doctor.

And she wasn't seventeen years old anymore.

"I had cancer. They took out part of my lung. But they did chemo, it's been two years, and it's over. So now they gotta go looking for something else. That's the way this life works, right?" He spread his hands, palms up. "That's it. Nothing to fuss over."

"I don't fuss," she said quietly. It was the kind of news she'd half expected. What she hadn't expected was the dazed feeling that suddenly dropped over her like a shroud. "I was raised by a man who doesn't tolerate fussing."

"What about your mother?" He gave a slight smile. "After you moved in with her, did you two get to fussing?"

"There was a brief honeymoon. After that we stayed out of each other's way until I moved. And then she moved." She met his eyes. "Dad, whatever your medical problem turns out to be, you need to…" She took a small step closer. "I hope you'll get the treatment you need as soon as you can. I can be as much help to Jack as you would be, and Iris is taking to the horses and calves like a duck to…" She smiled wistfully. "Like a thirteen-year-old girl to horses and calves."

"You think she might—"

Behind her the door opened, and a moment later Jack's voice filled the kitchen. "Iris, what's that I smell?"

"Calf poop? It's all over me."

"Nope. Can't smell calf crap anymore. But I can smell chili."

"I'll eat anything," Iris said. "I'm *totally* famished."

The snow was still falling, but the wind had let up, and Jack was able to haul fresh hay and set it out in a shelter belt near the calving shed while Lily rode the pasture. She found two cows giving birth in a small copse of ponderosa pine, and a third cleaning her new calf. The baby had already been licked dry and was almost ready to try out its legs. Once the two births had proved to be normal she made the rounds a second time before following the tractor back to the barn.

She'd said nothing to Jack about the talk she'd had with her father, and he hadn't asked. There was a kind of intimacy in working together yet separately on familiar tasks, sharing seamlessly, knowing when to reach in and when to wait. It was the same with the weight of her silence. It helped that he knew what she should have known all along, helped even more that he was waiting for her to speak of it.

He walked her to the house, took her hand when they reached the door and kissed her. They were both tired, but he left her with an option.

"My door is always open."

She squeezed his hand and answered with a kiss before she went inside. Tired as she was, a hot shower was all she wanted or needed. But she couldn't sleep, and she realized the question was not what she wanted or needed but whom.

So she went to him, greeted his dog, opened his door and found darkness inside. Quietly she slipped out of her jacket, pulled off her boots and set them beside his. She climbed up on the bench below the loft and peeked over the edge. By the light coming through the narrow window she could see his black hair against the white pillowcase. She wanted to share that pillow with him. That would be enough.

She took off her jeans and started to peel off her T-shirt, then thought better of it and kept her socks on, as well. Cold feet against his legs would be the rudest awakening. She took care not to jostle him as she climbed into the bed. He was on call for her father's cows, and he needed his sleep. She slid under his blankets without tugging or touching or declaring herself in any way.

He turned and took her in his arms. "You're overdressed."

"I was trying not to wake you up."

"Mmm." He kissed her gently as he tucked his hand under her shirt and slid it slowly up her back. "I'd almost given up on you."

"I tried not to come."

"Keep trying." He moved his hand from her back to her breast, brushed his thumb across her nipple and whispered, "It'll be that much better when you do."

And, oh, it was. He played one nipple with his thumb while he suckled the other through her soft cotton shirt until both breasts ached almost unbearably. Almost. He drew back just as she was about to clutch his head to her and hold him until the exquisite aching turned her inside out.

He hooked his leg across her hips and pressed his penis to her mons. He rotated his hips, stirring her as she heated up. She skinned her shirt over her head, freeing breasts that had surely expanded by a cup size, raised her shoulders off the bed and drew a deep breath. Her breasts lifted themselves to him like flowers to the sun. He teased them with laving tongue and nipping teeth and kneading lips, pressing harder on the fulcrum of her pelvis.

She dropped her shoulders back to free her hands for touching, but he allowed only the briefest contact with the slippery, satiny head of his penis before he slid down along her body, kissed her belly, grabbed the elastic band with his teeth and pulled her bikinis out of his way so he could drive her to distraction. He took her breasts in hand while he explored her most intimate secrets with his mouth.

Her body's rising need distracted her from putting up any resistance to its response. He was able to coax her legs farther apart with simple nudging, able to uncover more sensitivity, more vulnerability, more yearning. He pushed her up and up and up and over the low bar, giving her a solo takeoff before slipping into the seat he'd claimed as his and joining her on the run-up to the high bar, the one he was uniquely equipped to help her clear, to clear with her, and then to push her over again and again.

Long after they'd worn each other out they held fast to one another, legs entwined, arms embracing, hands possessing any part that drew them, for there was nothing to be held back. They were now entrusted to each other.

It felt like a miracle.

"My father had cancer." Lily paused—for affirmation, maybe denial, she wasn't sure—but he gave neither, which annoyed her more than any response would have. "So what's the big secret?"

"What do you mean?"

"Why didn't he tell me?" No answer. "Why wouldn't *you* tell me?"

"Sounds like you two had a little talk."

She stiffened. "Big secrets, little talks, everybody's safely tucked away inside."

"And nobody wins." He tucked his arm beneath her head and drew her close. "He talks about you a lot, Lily. You and Iris. Made it sound like he heard from you pretty regular and all was forgiven."

"All what?"

"Whatever drove you away. His drinking, I figured."

"When he found out I was pregnant he went nuts. Said he was going to shoot my boyfriend if he didn't marry me. *Marry me?* I was seventeen, Jack. A very inexperienced, terribly naive seventeen. I didn't know much about sex, and I didn't like what I'd seen of marriage. I wouldn't have married Cody even if he hadn't run like a scared buck."

"Buck?"

"Rabbit," she said. "The males are bucks. I raised rabbits once, remember?"

"I was a scared buck once, too. Part Indian, remember?"

"Did you run?"

"No. Hell, no. I was crazy about the woman, and I wanted to be with her. I just didn't know how to go about it."

"But you cowboyed up."

"That was all I knew how to do. Cowboy first,

everything else came after. Doesn't every woman want her own genuine bad-to-the-bone cowboy? I played it to the hilt."

She had no comment.

"So Mike was gonna shoot the boyfriend, huh?"

She laughed. "Scared?"

"Yeah. Mike scares me some. In his mind, illness and weakness are one and the same. If he takes a drink, he's weak. He'd rather be dead than weak."

"But he *did* take a drink."

"He had to be hurtin' pretty bad." He was quiet for a moment. "He put me to work before I quit drinking. I know it wasn't easy for him havin' me around at first. He didn't get after me. He just walked the walk."

"Were you with him when he had his surgery?"

"He didn't want me there, didn't want anyone there. But he couldn't get rid of me."

"I'm glad."

Again they let the silent moments pass.

Finally she asked, "Do you think it's spread?" She gave him a beat or two, no more. "*Do* you?"

"What *I* think don't mean nothin'. It's what *he* thinks."

She pressed her face to his chest, and he held her. She bathed his skin in warm breath and welcome tears.

"Oh, God, talk about weakness." Her voice was strong, almost heated. "I didn't know I had this in me. There's nothing to cry about, is there? Not yet, anyway."

"It's okay to cry."

She went small and timid. "It doesn't bother you?"

"Sure it does. I want to fix it, and I can't. All I can do is—"

"Hold me."

"That I can do." His arms enfolded her, and he whispered, "That I can do."

Lily had to dunk her face in cold water the next morning, so red and puffy were her eyes. A little makeup and her favorite blue sweater went a long way toward improving both look and outlook. And then Iris had to go padding into the kitchen on bare feet, looking tousled and sleepy and so little-girlish it made her mother's heart ache.

But sentimentality never earned a girl any scholarships.

"Why aren't you dressed for school?"

"With all this snow?" Iris looked horrified. "They can't possibly have school today."

"Oh, yes, they can." Lily forked bacon onto a paper towel to drain and turned off the stove. "According to the radio the buses are running late this morning, but they're running. You only get one snow day per storm."

"But I worked all day yesterday. That was no snow day. Snow days are supposed to be like vacation. No way am I getting on a bus this morning." Iris dragged a chair away from the kitchen table and plunked herself down like a sack of meal. "And don't give me that *ranch kid* shizzle. Kids don't have to work like that. We have laws."

"Parents have laws, too. There's one against truancy."

The opening back door drew Lily's head around.

"Do I smell coffee? I'll trade you my—" Jack poked his head beyond the alcove as he shed his black parka. "Hey, Iris, you skipping school today? I've got a calf out there needs some attention." He glanced at Lily. "Scours."

Lily groaned.

"Scour?" Iris scowled. "Like, scrub?"

"Scours is calf diarrhea," Lily said.

Jack was cowboy blunt. "And there's nothing slicker than a calf with the runs. You gotta wrestle 'em down and pour the recipe down their throats. You can handle it. Call in sick and dress for—"

"What time is the bus coming?" Iris said with a dramatic sigh.

"Be ready for whenever," Lily put in. "What do you want for breakfast? I've got—"

"Nothing." Lily gave her the *try again* look. "Okay, toast with peanut butter."

"Sounds good. I'll take mine with bacon and eggs," Jack said.

"Blech," Iris grumbled as she fled the kitchen.

"You do the toast and I'll do the eggs." Jack turned the faucet on and reached for the Lava soap. "Mike's doing better this morning."

Lily reached deep into the bread bag, noting she was due to make a run to the store. "I thought he was still in bed."

"He fired up the Allis and fed the cows."

"She's always been his favorite," Lily said of the old Allis-Chalmers tractor. "But do you think he ought to be operating heavy machinery? I mean, he's—"

"It's *his* machinery." Jack was looking for the towel Lily had taken down from the hook next to the sink. She handed him a clean one but didn't let go when he took it, and his smile acknowledged a growing connection that had little to do with the towel and everything to do with the gesture. "He seems okay this morning."

"Isn't he on some kind of medication?"

"He knows what he's doing."

She wasn't ready to let go of her end of the towel or the soft look in his eyes, meant for her alone. "I woke up and you were gone," she said quietly. "Why didn't you wake me? I can always help."

"You were a sleeping beauty this morning. I felt guilty just thinking about waking you up." His smile warmed his eyes and her whole face. "Maybe because I wasn't thinking about getting you out of bed."

"I wasn't—"

"Hey."

They started like two daydreamers, and the towel fell on Lily's bare feet.

"Is that the only towel in the house?" Iris drawled, mimicking her mother's usual *what-are-you-up-to?* tone. Lily had to laugh.

"The only one in the kitchen." Jack bent down and swept the towel off Lily's foot, then came up grinning at her. "Flip you for it."

"All yours." She waved the offer away.

"Oh. My. God." Iris planted her hands on her hips. "Who are you, lady, and what have you done with my mother?"

"What?" Lily feigned innocence. Not that it wasn't real at the moment, but the moment had its mixed undertones. "We're making breakfast here."

"Well, I've got a bad case of bed hair. No diarrhea, but I could still use some attention." She took her seat at the table. *"Mother."*

Jack was cracking nothing but eggs.

"No problem." Lily loaded up the toaster oven, pressed the button and turned to the table. *"Daughter."*

"I should have braided it last night." Iris handed Lily a hairbrush and gave a smug smile. "All yours." She brandished a hand mirror. "This is all mine." She squared her shoulders and positioned the mirror. "I've got my eye on you."

Lily went after Iris's tangled hair the way she always did when time was limited. No nonsense, all business.

"Ouch!"

Lily withdrew momentarily. "We women have to suck it up for beauty's sake."

"Beauty who? I just want it— Ow!" Iris adjusted the mirror as Lily freed the brush from a tangle. "I'm watching you, Mom. You've got that farmer's-wife-with-a-carving-knife look in your eye."

"Your hair is so thick and..." Lily scowled at the brush. Clearly it was the wrong tool for the job. "...thick and lovely, it's hard to do it justice without a little elbow grease."

"Grease is so yesterday," Iris quipped. "My hair is thick and it's tangled, but you don't have to go after it like you're raking weeds."

"We don't have much time, and I still have to—"

"Can I try?" Jack set a plate of toast with peanut butter in front of Iris. "I'm pretty good with a currycomb, but it's my brush work that turns horse hair into silk."

"*Horse* hair!" Iris protested.

"I just practice on horses, but my dream is to go into business fixing girls' hair someday. Cowboy Jack's *Salon*. Figure with a gig like that I'll get my own TV show." He winked at Lily. "Goodbye calving, hello curling."

Lily rolled her eyes and handed him the brush.

"Do you mind?" he asked Iris.

"Let's see your best brush stroke."

"Patience," he said as he put brush to hair. "That's the secret."

Lily watched him show her up. He took all the pains and gave none. Either that or Iris was faking somebody out.

"Is it more like a mane or a tail?" Iris asked her cowboy stylist.

"It's like my daughter's hair. She's tenderheaded, too."

His answer seemed to give her pause. After a moment she asked gently, "Do I look like her?"

"You're both girls. Both pretty."

Iris held up the hand mirror, angling it until they could both see his reflection beside hers.

"Do I look like I could be your daughter?"

"Looks can be deceiving," Jack said into the mirror. He glanced up at Lily.

She shrugged.

He looked back to the mirror. "It's the way people look at each other. That's what makes them family." He smiled. "That's the way I see it."

"You mean, the actual look in their eyes?" Iris said.

"That, too." He ran his hand over her hair, crown to nape. "Smooth as silk," he said.

"Can you teach Mom how to brush hair?"

He laughed. "I'd be a fool to touch that question."

"How are your braiding skills?" Lily put in.

"See what I mean?" Jack said to Iris. She nodded, and he looked up at Lily. "Pitiful compared to yours," he assured her as he stepped aside.

"Then I'll trade lessons with you." She caught him winking at Iris, and she couldn't help getting her game face on. "French, fishtail, or should we go Dutch?"

"Your call," he said to Iris. "I don't know what the hell she's talkin' about."

"That's the idea," Lily said with a grin.

Chapter Seven

"This is no good, Dad."

Lily took one look at the label on the bottle she found in the "special" cupboard above the refrigerator and shook her head. "You can't use just any old vinegar. How old is this stuff?"

"How long you been gone?" Mike was still working on his breakfast—moving the eggs and biscuits around on his plate—and watching her sort through the bottles and boxes of remedies, and ingredients for remedies, for various ailments. There were some for people, some for animals, some for both. "I think I've got some apple-cider vinegar in the pantry."

"*Raw* apple-cider vinegar. Organic." She stood on her toes on the kitchen step chair and reached for the top shelf. "I don't see any psyllium husk up here."

"You gotta have that?"

"I don't know. I just follow the recipe. I know you can't get stuff like that at Bailey's. I don't even know if you could find it in Glendive." She moved jars and bottles until she found something useful. "At least we have the right kind of clay powder."

"It's all been up there since you were here last. Does that clay get too old, too?"

"It shouldn't. It comes out of the ground. Literally as old as the hills. I think we've got enough of the basics here, but somebody should go over to Livingston or maybe, I don't know, someplace where we can stock up on scours-recipe ingredients." She handed the jar down to Jack, who was piling containers on the counter. "This clay is really good for your face."

"What's wrong with my face?"

"Anybody's face. If you're outdoors a lot, a clay mask is good for chapped skin. That's all I can find up here." She put her hand on his shoulder, and he helped her down. Not that she needed help, but she found herself enjoying his public attention at every turn, which was a little scary. But it was almost as good as his private attention. And that was perfect.

She smiled and put her hand on his clean-shaven cheek. "You look fine. I'm just sayin', I know a few things. I used to sell cosmetics. My mother got me started when I moved in with her." She turned to take inventory of the ingredients they'd assembled. "Helped put me through school," she said absently. "That and braiding hair."

"You can make a living braiding hair?"

"Not if that's all you do, but every little bit helps when you're trying to pay for college and day care. The Renaissance Festival was our best gig for hair braiding." She shrugged. "Anyway, this was my mother's recipe."

"Not your mother's, your grandmother's," her father said. "Your mother got it from my mother."

"Oh."

Every once in a while she tried to give her mother credit for something. It rarely stuck.

"But now it's yours," Mike said.

"Still, treating scours was Mom's job until it became mine. How many calves need to be treated?"

She was cracking eggs into a big ceramic bowl that had also been Grandma's. It really didn't matter how many critters would be served, since the scours recipe was designed for the bowl, and the bowl was always used to make the recipe. Well, that and enough batter to bake Grandma's Hot Milk Cake for a branding crew. Lily wondered whether she still remembered that recipe.

She had to. If she didn't, who would? Grandma's Hot Milk Cake was amazing. "After you left I just used the commercial stuff," her father was saying. "They don't like it much, do they, Jack?"

"No, but that's what most guys use." He glanced up from reading the label on the clay-powder jar and told Lily, "In answer to your question, we've got six so far."

"And we lose the real stubborn calves that won't take it," Mike said. "But if memory serves, they generally drink up this recipe like it came straight from their mama."

"It's a good thing I'm back, then," Lily said. And she meant it. Poor little poopy calves. "I'll write it down so you have it on file."

Mike pushed his plate away and leaned back in his chair. "Don't keep too much paper around. Fire hazard. I know every cow's history, every piece of equipment, every square foot of land and every kind of plant that grows on it. If I can't store it in my head it can't be too important."

"So the recipe isn't—"

"Oh, yeah, it's important, but seems like it's a woman thing. It went away with you, and now you brought it back." He gave her an odd look and added quietly, "I do keep a few important papers over at the bank."

She turned and took a pan of warm beef stock off the stove and added commercial calf electrolytes, along with the ingredients her father had finally remembered were stored in the least accessible cupboard in the kitchen.

"In a safe-deposit box?" Lily asked absently.

"Yup. The lawyer has copies, too. Anybody says to me, get your affairs in order, I can say I got the jump on him. Or her."

Lily turned, scowling. "I won't be saying—"

"My doctor's a *her,*" Mike continued as he rose from the table. "She ain't said it yet, so nothing to worry about."

"She's said you need tests."

"Yeah, and I've only spilled those beans on two people." He shifted his gaze from his daughter to his right-hand man. "Which was two too many, because they won't shut up about it. You notice I'm gettin' around pretty good since I caught up on my rest." He took several steady steps toward her. *"You notice?"*

"But the tests—"

"—can wait." He peered into the bowl. "Mmm, that looks good." He turned to Jack. "You ready to ride, rope and wrestle, McKenzie?"

"I was born ready."

He was born ready. Typical cowboy, Lily thought. Coming from Jack, the claim gave her goose bumps.

No matter what her father said about calves sucking up the recipe, treating them in the pasture wasn't an easy job, but with Jack doing the roping and Lily doing the feeding, it was almost fun. He only missed his first loop once, but she pounced on the chance to tease him after he'd laughed when one of her patients unloaded on her boots. Later she helped him pull another calf, check on the cows with healthy new calves that had been moved away from the sick ones, and hook CC up with her increasingly accepting adoptive mother.

It was late when they returned to the house for supper. Iris had already eaten with her grandfather, who was listening to her play "Für Elise" on the upright piano he had covered, turned to the wall and used as a bookshelf while Lily had been gone. Too tired to talk, Lily and Jack shared food and fatigue, feeling satisfied because they'd done a good day's work. They were becoming a team.

"Gotta get to bed," he said when they'd finished cleaning up their dishes.

She had to stand on her toes to reach the shelf where the casserole pan went, and as she did, she felt him close in behind her. Together with the word *bed,* his proximity made her quiver inside.

Ridiculous. She'd barely had enough energy to reach the top shelf of the cupboard. How could she be having a full-body quiver?

He slipped his arms around her waist and put his lips almost irresistibly close to her ear. "Are you going to try not to come tonight?"

"I don't know how you get by with so little sleep."

"I'm a day worker. No contract means no schedule." He nuzzled her neck. "I adjust."

"You're working day and night."

"Cowboy," he whispered. The scrape of his teeth on her neck sent a shiver all the way to her toes.

"I love…" She turned in his arms as Iris switched to the theme from *Arthur,* one of her other favorites. The word hung between them on a thread of expectancy. It surprised her. Probably scared him. She couldn't laugh it off, couldn't even muster a coy smile. She lowered her gaze. "…that movie."

"What movie?" She looked up quickly. "Yeah, I saw it. Took my kids. Charming drunk, that guy." He tapped her chin with his forefinger. "I wasn't like that."

"What *were* you like?"

"You know the answer to that. You've lived it." His smile seemed apologetic, a little sad. "You wouldn't like me when I'm drunk."

She slid her arms around his waist. Time to take both their minds off the past. "Well, I like you just fine *now,* cowboy."

He gave her a quick kiss. "I wouldn't have it any other way."

Iris was sitting on her bed, resting against a pile of pink-and-green pillows, nose in a book. She didn't look up when Lily walked into the room. Point taken. Lily had fallen short of too many expectations lately. Missing supper had apparently not only tipped the scales but toppled them.

But Lily ignored the stab of deserved guilt and sat down at the foot of the bed anyway. Caring for Iris took precedence over her own feelings. "How was that math quiz today?"

"Easy."

"What are you reading?"

Iris lifted the book—a Montana history—and then quickly slid it back into place behind her upraised knees.

"Is that for school?"

"It's for me."

"A little heavy for pleasure reading. So the subject drew you, huh?"

Ignoring the question, Iris said, "You've always said I could read whatever I wanted to."

"And you've always been a precocious reader.

I just wondered whether Montana is turning out to be—"

Iris finally looked up, eyes flashing. "You said it would be temporary."

"I said probably."

"You said you'd get a job and work for a while, save some money."

"We just got here, and I've already got my foot in the school doors."

"And you said after we saved some magic number of dollars we'd go back home and start over."

"Back home," Lily echoed. "You mean Minneapolis?"

"Duh. I've lived there all my life. Where else would home be?"

"Good point." No comment on the forbidden expression. From the look in Iris's eyes, it could have been worse. "The way you've taken to the horses and helped with the calves, I thought you were over the moving misery. I was rushing it. I'm sorry. I know you need time. I'm really proud of the way you—"

"Are you in love with Jack?"

"In love?" She hadn't seen that coming.

"Yeah, you know, that thing that makes people write silly songs and sappy poetry. I've never seen you like this."

"Like what?" *Duh.*

"Like, who *are* you? You're not my mother. My

mother never gets all gaga over a man. Of course, the guys you go out with are always such geeks, I don't know why you bother, but still..."

"What do you mean by gaga? What am I doing?" As soon as the question was out she realized how childish it sounded. Defensive. Dishonest. Guilty.

"You're just...*gaga*." The gestures were flying now. "Over the top. The goo-goo eyes, the way you laugh when he's around, the way you're not asking me what I've been doing every time I've been out of your sight for five minutes."

"I just asked you."

"Grandpa said they called you again to sub and you said you couldn't. You're supposed to be a teacher, Mom."

"Those calves have started dropping like crazy, plus the weather, plus the scours. I'm needed here."

Iris fell back against the pillows with a drawn-out groan. "If you marry him, we'll be stuck here."

"*Marry* him!" Iris's dramatic gesture gave Lily leave to laugh. "And I thought *I* was the one rushing *you*."

"Isn't that what you're supposed to do when you fall in love? Get married?" Iris sprang forward and leaned in, almost nose to nose. "Come on, Mom, I hear you singing those silly songs sometimes. And you teach poetry, for cripes sake."

"I like him." Smiling—probably blushing—Lily lifted one shoulder. "Okay, I like him a lot."

"And you didn't love my father at all. Not one little bit?" Iris looked her mother in the eye. Lily held her gaze until Iris gave in and looked down at the book in her lap. "You liked him," she said quietly. "You had to like him."

"I liked him." It was the best Lily had to offer. "I was very young."

"You always say that." Iris took a moment, clearly weighing her next move. "I like Jack, too," she said in the smallest voice she'd brought to the conversation so far. "I know when you're young, it's just a crush. You get over it, kinda like the flu. Which is comforting."

"I'll say."

"But if you fall in love with him, you'll never get over it. You've been waiting a long time, saving up. If he's the one..." She snapped the book shut. "And you're not *very young* anymore."

"I'm not *old*."

"You're ageless. You're *Mom*. You always have been. It's hard to believe you were ever my age." Iris waved her hand at the photographs dotting the room, images of the schoolgirl neither one of them could quite believe. "I've been looking at these pictures, and I see the resemblance, but…a younger cousin, maybe?"

"My God, you're making me feel like some tired old maid."

"You can't be an old maid if you've got a kid," Iris said as she tossed the book on the nightstand.

"Good point."

And then along came Iris's trademark I've-got-a-secret smile. "Actually, I found proof that a kid once lived in this house, that she started out as a baby and went through all the stages."

"Where? What kind of proof?"

"Pictures, of course. I found a box in the back of the closet."

Mom's picture box. Lily couldn't remember when she'd last seen it. She jerked her thumb over her shoulder. "*This* closet?"

Iris nodded toward the door. "The closet in the other room. The one you're using. Way in the back."

"What were you doing in there?"

"Exploring. That closet slants way down in back, and there's stuff like old record albums and baby toys in boxes." Iris scooted to the edge of the bed. "Wanna see? I want you to tell me about the people in the pictures."

No, Lily didn't want to see. It had been a long time since she'd thought about the people in those pictures.

But she owed her daughter some forebears. It wasn't about the past, per se. It was about the blood and the birthright that passed through them to their descendants. Iris didn't remember her grandmother. She had a mother in the flesh, and now she had a grandfather. The rest were names and select memories, pretty in pictures.

Lily was named for her mother's mother, Lily Greenwood, who could have counted on one hand the trips she'd taken beyond the Iowa state line. The box held five pictures of Grandma Lily and none of Grandpa Woody. There were a few pictures of groups of relatives and the usual holiday shots of kids. Lily was able to name most of them.

But it was Carrie Greenwood who stood out, even as a child. The camera loved Lily's beautiful mother, and when she was young she'd loved it right back.

By the time Carrie was about twelve, the images betrayed the growing restlessness that would become her driving force. In a group she was the one who moved just as the shutter clicked. She was off in a dream world for her school picture. And then she'd met Mike Reardon. He'd been an older man of some means, and he'd offered to take her to a place that was not Iowa. Lily didn't romanticize her parents' courtship as they sat together going through the photos, but she didn't want to prejudice Iris against her grandmother, either.

"Where is she now?" Iris asked, looking at the pale-haired girl in the school picture.

"The last I heard she was in Georgia, but that was years ago. She called on my birthday, said she'd finally met Mr. Right." Lily looked at the beautiful girl in the picture. *Who were you, Carrie Greenwood Reardon? Who are you now?* "I hope she's finally happy."

"You'd never do that to me. I know you wouldn't. Even if I *was* an accident."

"Oh, sweetie, you're no accident." Lily reached for her daughter's hand. "You're the best thing that ever happened to me. You were meant to be." She lifted the picture for another look. "I don't know what makes my mother tick—don't even know if she's still ticking—but I'm glad you found these. Seeing them now…" She took another picture from the pile they'd made on the bed. "They look different to me. They don't make me feel…left out." She took the picture and looked at it more closely. "My mother. For better or worse, she's my mother. And I'm…" She took the last pictures out of the wooden box—the big eight-by-tens—and noticed a manila envelope with a brass fastener at the bottom of the box. "What's in here?"

"I didn't look at everything."

Lily waited quietly for her answer.

"Letters," Iris said, her tone confessional. "But I didn't read them. I saw what they were, and I…" Lily pulled a handful of mail from the big envelope. "…didn't take them out."

The letters were addressed to her mother at a post-office box in Lowdown. There were no return addresses, but the envelopes bore twenty-year-old postmarks. Lily looked up at Iris.

Iris lifted one slender shoulder. "I guess Grandma had a good friend in Minneapolis before she moved there."

"I thought you didn't take them out."

"*Of their envelopes.* At first I thought, 'Minneapolis. They're from Mom.' But then I did the math."

"Would you have read them if they *were* from me?"

"No, of course I…probably might not have. Fortunately, I'm good at math." Iris stared at the envelope. "We don't have secrets. You're always saying what's yours is mine."

"We have privacy. Letters are private. You would have asked me, and I would have…*probably might have* said yes." Lily looked closely at Iris. Her daughter wanted someone else. Not instead of her mother, but in addition. She wanted family. "Your father isn't a secret," Lily said. "And I'm sorry, but I don't know where *he* is, either."

"Do you wish you did?"

"Only because you do."

Iris nodded toward the pile of twenty-year-old letters. As hard as they'd both been staring at them, it was a wonder they hadn't burst into flames. "So would you read these if they were mine?"

"Not unless I knew you were in serious trouble and I was trying to figure out how I could help you," Lily said. "Otherwise, no."

"Are you going to read these? Grandma might be in trouble. Seriously. These might give you a clue." When that got no response, Iris went in for the kill. "She might be dead."

"Either way, I couldn't help her, so what good would it do?"

"I don't know. But those letters could be interesting. Maybe you've got family you don't even know about or something."

"Have you been watching reality shows again?"

"We don't get cable here." Iris smiled. "The pictures are really sweet. Why didn't you name me Carrie?"

"The truth is, your grandmother suggested Iris. And I loved it. I love irises and lilies, and I love the way they go together."

"Maybe I'll name my kid Carrie. If I decide to

have a kid." She gave her mother a sassy smile. "Or if it's *meant to be*."

After Iris went to her room, Lily sat in the middle of her bed and stared at the closet door. What would be the point in reading the letters? They'd been written by a man. Had to be. But who was he, and where had her mother met him? And when? And what difference could it possibly make now? Who cared anymore, really?

Her father, maybe? If Mom had had an affair and Dad found out about it, that would explain some of his behavior. And if he didn't know, why add insult to injury?

Mike Reardon was a sick man, maybe a dying one. The last thing he needed to concern himself with was Lily's mother's indiscretions. *Possible* indiscretions. Nobody doubted that Lily's mother had deserted her father, and that her father...

What if Mike Reardon *wasn't* her father? What if her father was the letter writer?

Then Mike's rejection of his pregnant teenage daughter suddenly became more complicated than Lily thought. Complicated, but still not forgivable.

And what were the odds that somewhere there was a man walking around who didn't even know he had a daughter, much less a granddaughter, living in Montana?

Could be as much as fifty-fifty.

Maybe she was trying to mend the wrong fence.

She'd never been one to shy away from the truth, but whatever the truth was, it wouldn't change the fact that when you got right down to it, Mike and Iris Reardon were all she had. And if truth be told...

The truth—*some* truth—was in those letters.

Chapter Eight

Jack wasn't surprised he'd had no visitor last night, but the level of his disappointment *did* surprise him. He'd felt the cold wind biting into his face when he'd done his 4:00 a.m. rounds, felt it steal his breath and pinch his heart. He'd summoned the memory of riding with Lily, being her shield from the cold, feeling needed in ways that made a man more than a mere man. He had power. He could be fire-maker and food-bringer and family-provider. With nothing more than his body he could keep a woman warm.

He could keep a woman.

He could make her his woman, and she could count on him to be her man.

Could a cowboy do all that? A cow*man* definitely could, but a cowboy? Jack had nothing to show for his thirty-five years but a good horse, a small trailer and a pair of calloused hands. He'd learned some hard lessons, fixed a few things, but there were some mistakes that couldn't be fixed. They were like calluses. You lived with them. The hard places protected the tender spots.

He rubbed his thumb over the back of CC's oversize ear. "I have a feeling that crabby ol' cow will take you this morning without restraints. You willing to risk it?"

"Good question. We never know what's worth the risk, do we?"

Jack turned his smile from the calf to the woman standing outside the stall. "Spoken like a true female."

Lily laughed. "How so?"

"I ask one question and you answer with another." He braced one hand on his knee and pushed to his feet.

"This time the calf is the one taking the risk." She came to him smiling, and he kissed her for it. "That's why it's such a good question. So how much skin are *you* willing to put into the game?"

"That's an even better question." He slid his arms around her and drank in the merriment dancing in her eyes. "And you know the answer, but I'm more than happy to repeat it for you. I'm big on demonstrating instead of just bragging my-self up."

"The *calf* risks getting kicked away from the tit."

"Teat." He grinned. "I could get kicked just as easy."

"But the calf would also go hungry." She kissed him back. "Double jeopardy."

"I went hungry last night."

"Did it keep you awake?"

He laughed and shook his head. "I slept like a baby until Hula woke me up for four o'clock rounds."

"Any problems?"

"Nope. The females are handling their labors just fine." He took a lead rope down from a hook. "You women have the power. You know it, too. All we males have are questions. Some good, some stupid. You throw one out there, you've got a fifty-fifty chance of getting the answer you want."

"Funny you should say that. I found myself up against a fifty-fifty proposition last night. I need some advice."

"That's a tough one for a guy who's working for wages. Cowboys don't advise."

"How about friends?"

"Tell you what. You help me with this little experiment I'm about to do, I'll lend you my good ear."

"You have a bad one?"

"If I turn the right one your way, you know I've lost interest." He tugged on his right earlobe. "Busted eardrum."

"What do you need?"

"That bovine bitch outside." He handed her the lead rope. "Cross-tied in the alley. I don't want her boxed in. I'm going to find Hula."

"Won't the dog make her nervous?"

"I don't know. I'm hoping the dog will make a mother out of her."

Lily had the cow in position when he returned with the dog. He called her to the barn door and handed her Hula's leash. "I'll tell you when to bring her inside. I want you to tie her right here." He pointed to the metal handle of a box-stall door about ten feet from where the cow stood. "If the cow gets away from me, save my dog."

"I think you're crazy," Lily said as she followed instructions.

"And don't you ever forget it."

He gave the cow a couple of chances to take CC for the first time without hobbles, but she sidled away. Her kick wasn't serious, but it was enough to dissuade the calf.

"Okay, bring in the enforcer," Jack called out. He put the hungry calf near the burgeoning source of milk—damn, that bag had to be painful—and backed out of the way.

With a hand signal Jack had the tethered dog baring her teeth. The cow's protective instinct kicked in immediately. Her focus was on the dog. The calf was allowed to tuck under her bag and drink her fill.

"I pronounce you mother and daughter," Jack said when the feeding was over. Hula got her breakfast, the cow got a fresh bale of hay, and CC was adopted.

"I'm feeling unusually wise now, woman." Jack took a seat on a small stack of hay bales and patted the space beside him. "Come tell me your problem."

"Are you feeling serious?"

"I'm giving you my left ear. How much more serious can I be?" He patted the prickly bale again.

With a dubious glance she took her seat and started talking.

"Iris found a box in the back of the closet in the spare room. I haven't seen that box since Mom lived here. She kept family pictures in it, *her* side of the family, from when she was a child and even before. The first time I found the box— stumbled across it nosing around, just the way Iris did—Mom took it away and told me to stay out of her stuff.

"A few days later she sat me down with it and told me about the people who had been part of her life, who had come before me. It felt funny, hearing her talk about these strange people as though she had belonged with them at one time. She wasn't like that. She never wanted to belong, not anywhere or *to* anyone. I'd try to find ways to be like her, look like her, please her. I made pictures and little presents for her, and she'd put them in a drawer. She was always about half here and half somewhere else."

She paused, took a breather, but he knew there was more. He'd said he could listen, but he hadn't imagined he would see himself as a player in the kind of situation she described. Worse, he could see his own kids in Lily.

"I felt guilty about it," she said. "Back then, and maybe even now."

"You?" He frowned. "Why?"

"Maybe her two halves could have been one whole person if it wasn't for me." She shrugged. "Of course that's ridiculous, but she probably needed to leave sooner, regardless."

"I wouldn't say it's ridiculous. Feelings are feelings. There's nothing wrong about whatever you felt then."

"But I need to get over it, right?"

"I wouldn't say *that,* either. That would be drifting into the advice department."

"I stayed with her for almost two years after Iris was born."

"And then you got your own place?"

"She got *her* own place. Out of town. Out of *state*. And I guess for her it was 'out of sight, out of mind.'" Her quick laugh brightened the memory. "Best thing that ever happened to me. Mom paid the rent three months in advance before she left. I'd already started taking classes at a community college, and the counselor helped me fill out applications for the local university and for financial aid. I knew what I wanted, and I was on my way." She shook her head, sighing. "And now I'm back where I started. Full circle."

"That's not a bad thing," he said with a smile. "Some people believe that's how we live. You've got your timeline. Indian people have their circle."

"Is that from your mother's side or your father's?"

"Little bit of both. My mother's part Lakota. My father was Métis. His grandparents came here from Canada." He tipped his head to one side, curious. "What did Iris think of the pictures in that box?"

"She was interested in who they were. I think I answered her questions pretty well. I'm surprised I remembered the names. Maybe because they seemed important to my mother when she gave them to me."

"And now you've given them to your daughter."

"It isn't much, but I guess it's something. Maybe we'll try to track them down sometime. You can do that now on the internet." She laughed. "If we had internet."

"My grandfather taught me to sing the names of my ancestors. 'The old ones,' he called them. He was an old guy himself, I thought. Course, I was pretty young. He didn't talk much unless he was telling a story, but damn, he could sing. Hell of a fiddle player, too. He wanted to teach me, but I didn't catch on the way my brother did. Hey, Iris sure can play that piano. You play?"

"I was never as good as she is." She gave him a second look. "You have a brother?"

"*Had.* He was killed in a car accident with my father."

"Both at once? Oh, Jack, I'm so—"

"Don't be sorry. It happened a long time ago. You don't owe me an apology, and I don't need pity."

"How old were you?"

"About Iris's age." *About* sounded slippery. He knew exactly how old he'd been. "Twelve. They were with me twelve years. They left a few pictures and a lot of memories." He rubbed the corner of his forehead. "And scars."

"Scars?"

"See this right here?" He moved his fingers away from the scar that had taken a chunk out of his eyebrow. "We were cleaning up the yard, Joe and me, and he bet me he could balance the rake in the palm of his hand. He'd seen a guy do it. And, hell, he had it there for a second or two."

"It fell on you?" She touched the scar gingerly, as though it might still be tender. "Could have taken your eye out."

"But it didn't." He chuckled. *"Could have taken your eye out.* That's exactly what my mom said. Joe felt so bad, he let me use his catcher's mitt every day until I got the stitches out. I got some more up here." He bowed his head, reached for her hand and pushed her fingertips into his hair, searching for the little railroad track on his scalp. "Feel that? We made little rock-throwing catapults."

"Could have taken out your whole memory."

"Whenever I can't think of something, I scratch my head right there and Joe's spirit fills me in."

"You must forget things a lot, because you've rubbed yourself bald here. Good thing you have thick hair."

"I gotta start writing stuff down. Spare the hair."

A quiet moment passed.

"There was something else in the box," she said finally. "I don't remember seeing it, but maybe it was there last time I..." She drew a deep breath and released it in a sigh. "A big envelope full of letters to my mother."

"From?"

"I don't know." She lifted one shoulder. "A man."

"You read them?"

"No. Not yet. I just...know it was a man." She turned to him and confessed in a small voice, "I sort of want to read them."

"Why?"

"That's what I want to know. Why?"

"You'd ask a man for advice about something like that?" He shook his head. "Honey, that's a no-brainer."

"You said you didn't give advice."

"I don't. And you don't need any. If you don't burn those things right away, you'll read them. Just remember, you can't *un*read them."

"So you're saying I shouldn't read them."

"Nope." He leaned forward and planted his elbows on his knees. "I'm just listening." Being a wise man was damned hard work.

"Well, you're not helping."

"Iris saw the letters?" Lily nodded, and he said, "She found the box. Maybe she read them."

"She didn't." Then she asked, "My mother cheated on my father, didn't she."

"Would it help if she did? Make it easier for

you to forgive Mike?" He laid his hand on her knee. "If it would…"

"If it would, then your advice would be…"

"Just givin' you something to chew on."

She covered his hand with hers. "Dad wants me to go to a co-op meeting. Do you ever go to those meetings?"

"Nah, Mike's the rancher. I'm just a ranch hand. We don't do meetings."

"Would you?" She squeezed his hand. "If I asked?"

"It might not be long before…before you don't have to ask. Before you just tell me to go and I'll go."

She questioned him with a look. What was he suggesting? It might not be long before…*what?*

"You're gonna own this place one of these days. You won't have any trouble finding a buyer for it if that's what you want to do, but you could run it yourself."

"This is Dad's place."

He nodded. "Right now he needs a partner. That's why he wants you to go to one of those meetings. What he's been doing in the last few years, what he's been building here with his neighbors…" He nodded. "You gotta know it was hard for him to get it going, but he believes in it. He's got me convinced. Finishing out the steers on grass is better for everybody. No growth hormones, no drugs, no feedlots, no stress." He smiled. "Good meat."

"Go to a meeting with me." She smiled back. "It'll be our first date."

"We haven't had a date yet? I thought…"

She gave him the stink eye.

"That doesn't count?"

"That *does* count, but not as a date."

"It counts with me, too." He turned his palm to hers. "I'll sit through a co-op meeting with you if you'll go somewhere with me. I want my kids to meet you." He chuckled. "They think I'm a hermit."

"They do?"

"Becky calls me Old Man Turtle because I carry my house with me. She says I'll never get another wife unless I get a bigger trailer."

"She wants you to get another wife?"

"Becky's been worried about me ever since Edie remarried."

"Because you're alone?"

"Because I live in a horse trailer." He lifted one shoulder. "Which is all I need, but she's at that age, you know? It matters what her friends think. So I don't take the trailer up to Wolf Point anymore."

"Wolf Point?"

He challenged her with a look. *Something wrong with Wolf Point?*

"Well, you know what they say around here. If you come to a sign that says 'Welcome to Wolf Point,' you've gone too far."

"Yeah. You're in Indian Country." He grinned. "We say that about the sign that says 'Welcome to Canada.' The Métis couldn't get recognized up there until the 1980s. We got recognized here as Chippewa or Cree. Or both. This side of the border, it's all about Indian-blood quantum." He caught her gaze with his own. Now he was serious. "So tell me…have *you* gone too far, Lily?"

"With you?" She shook her head. "I've come further with you than I have with anyone. Ever."

"So Wolf Point isn't out of the question?"

"The co-op meeting is tonight." She squeezed his hand again. "I'm good for Wolf Point anytime."

Chapter Nine

"If I have to go to this thing, you're going, too." Jack cut the last band of twine off a bale of alfalfa, gave it a good kick and inhaled the scent of summer hay. "You know how I feel about meetings."

"It's people you know, people you've worked for." Mike stood by watching his cows follow their noses, their black-and-white faces headed in his direction. Jack could tell he wasn't feeling too well by the way he was keeping his hands in his jacket pockets. No work gloves. Sure sign. "They mostly talk weather, grass and cattle," Mike went on absently. "Be good for you."

Jack took up his post at his boss's side and

watched herringbone clouds scudding across blue sky. "What's good for me is keeping my head down and my mouth shut. You do that at any kind of a meeting, people start jabbing you with their damned elbows."

"I can only recall doing that to you once. And this is a different kind of meeting." Mike kicked at a dried-up cow pie with the toe of his boot. "I made an appointment for the damn CT scan they want to do on me. You go to this meeting for me, I'll keep the appointment."

Jack turned his head, hiked one eyebrow and stared.

"All right, let me put it to you this way. I'm scared. I wasn't before, but now I am. So I don't want to go nowhere. I'd be content to take a bottle with me out to the pasture and watch the sun set. But I won't do that. I'll get the damn X-rays."

"You want me to go with you?"

"I don't need anybody holding my hand. Ain't *that* damn scared," Mike grumbled. "I want you to go to that meeting with Lily. I want her to see what the High Plains Grass-fed Beef Co-op is all about."

Jack lifted one shoulder. "Why don't you just tell her?"

"I'm not the co-op. I'm the man who kicked her out when she told me she was pregnant." Mike shook his head and waved the confession away with a bony hand. "Used to be, anyway. I'm not that man anymore, but I was a son of a bitch back then. 'No daughter of Mike Reardon's…'" He shook his finger and mimicked his former self in what was supposed to pass for a booming voice. It came off reedy and hoarse. "Her mother'd already up and left. Never gave me a reason, but I figured she had somebody else waitin' for her. What the hell, she was young and pretty, and I was…"

"An old son of a bitch."

"Not all the time." Mike stepped back to make way for a cow who had her eye on a bit of alfalfa that was almost as green as the day it was cut. "I wasn't half bad-lookin' when I married her, and I didn't drink that much then. Went to church, got on the school board…" He glanced away. "Even though she never gave me reason to worry, I had it in my head that Lily was gonna turn out like her mother. She told me she was pregnant—hell, I didn't even know she had a boyfriend—and I told her to get married or go live with her mother. Seemed like I didn't even know my own kid."

"You must've been pretty busy going to church and hittin' those school-board meetings." Jack smiled sadly. "When your wife left you, Lily's mother also left her. Lily was pretty young."

"I know they had a little talk before she left. All Lily told me was that she wanted to be here, but I don't think her mother gave her much choice.

We just went on with our lives. She had her chores and her riding. She liked school and all her activities. Played piano. She was real busy. I didn't think she had time to get herself in trouble."

"Ah, Mike." Jack shook his head and gave a humorless chuckle. "I've got no room to talk about being a father, and girls are pretty hard to figure anyway. But you've gotta be proud of her. Look how far she's come on her own."

"I know. I know." Mike reached for the cow's withers. She permitted a little scratching and then sidled away. "She can do whatever she wants with this place when I'm gone, but it'll take some time for her to figure it out. She'll need your help."

"You just said you weren't goin' nowhere." Mike didn't take the bait. "All right, if you don't feel like going, I'll make you another offer. I'll take Lily to the damn meeting and throw in supper, but you gotta do me a solid in return." He waited for Mike to look up. "Don't push me."

"You know I don't push."

"No, you never have, not since I've known you. When I take on a job, I do it your way, no question. But I decide what jobs I take on and who I work for. No question."

Mike nodded.

"It might sound prideful, but that's all I've got right now. I'm a piece of work, I admit, but I'm under reconstruction."

"You're a good man, Jack. I couldn't ask for a better..." Mike caught himself and smiled. "Couldn't ask for better."

"As long as you're paying me by the hour, I'll try to stay awake." Jack punched Mike's scrawny shoulder. "JK." He grinned. "Just kidding."

The monthly High Plains Grass-fed Beef Co-op meeting was held in the basement of the Presbyterian Church. Not much had changed since Lily had attended services as a child with her dad. She remembered her mother going along in the early days, but by the time Lily was about seven or eight, her mother's church days were over. Lily showed Jack the room where she'd gone to Sunday school and later taught classes. He didn't claim to be much of a churchgoer, but he said he'd take another crack at it for the privilege of seeing her in her Sunday best.

"You already have," she told him.

He grinned. "You were born on a Sunday?"

She tried to play-punch him in the stomach, but he sucked it in, grabbed her hand and planted a succulent kiss on her mouth right there in her old Sunday-school room. She wondered how guilty she looked when they emerged and found five of the six co-op members seated around a folding table in the parish hall. They seemed more surprised to see Jack there than Lily.

"Where's Mike?" Jeanie Taylor wanted to know. Jeanie seemed a little wary of Lily, probably because her daughter had been Lily's best friend when she'd gotten pregnant. Molly had had to sneak off with the pickup to drive Lily to the bus stop, and they'd shared some last laughs over the notion that Molly's mother was afraid Lily's problem would rub off. "Your father never misses a meeting unless there's something wrong," Jeanie said.

"Even when he's calving? That's hard to believe. He sent me to go in his place so he could do what he does best."

"Still calving?" Jeanie glanced back and forth between Jack and Lily. "We were all done before the storm hit. Are you having any trouble?"

"Not a bit," Lily said. She looked up at Jack. "Dad's put together quite a team."

"Vern thinks we'll be able to afford to hire more help this year."

Lily couldn't resist linking arms with Jack. "This cowboy's taken."

"I see that." Jeanie gave him a thoughtful glance. "It's hard to come by the real thing these days."

"Looks like they're ready to start," Jack told Lily, touching his hat brim with one hand, the small of her back with the other. "Let's go."

Lily and Jack sat at one end of the table. He moved his chair a few inches back from the table, and she almost followed suit, but she decided it was his way of saying he had her back, and she liked that. She was there to learn.

She was there because she was her father's daughter.

And so she attended to her father's business. Everyone agreed on the need to expand, but only two of the members were convinced that Rocking R neighbor Clinton Tyree would be a worthwhile convert. Like most of the old-timers, Tyree was set in his ways, more interested in adding new boots to his fence-line display than trying out new ways—or reviving old ones—to produce beef. Tyree ran the biggest cow-calf operation in northeastern Montana, and his favorite comeback for the co-op members who'd tried to convert him was, "Better ranching through chemistry." He'd been using growth hormones and antibiotics for forty years or more. "The system ain't broke, and neither am I," he always said.

With drought in the Midwest and poor corn crops two years running, grass-fed beef was gaining respect in the cattle business and popularity among consumers. If the co-op couldn't supply enough beef to meet that demand, their wholesaler would soon be looking for a more productive source. Phil Jensen offered to show Tyree his next steer check. "The proof is in the digits,"

Phil said, and they tabled the discussion until that could happen.

Lily took out her ever-present purse-size notebook and jotted down a few notes during the discussion of inspections and certification. If her father asked for a report, she would have one ready. She'd said she was going to earn her keep, but the truth was, the discussion was actually turning out to be interesting. She'd grown up watching buyers load Rocking R calves into their trucks, and she knew they were headed for feedlots followed by slaughter. Growth hormones, antibiotics and corn were all part of the process. It wasn't until she'd become a mother that she'd become a careful reader of food labels. She liked what she was hearing at this meeting, partly because it was about producing healthy food, and partly because Jack's claim that the co-op was her father's "baby" was beginning to sink in.

Her father had started something pretty darn big.

"Heard you was back home, Lily," Phil Jensen called out to her as she approached the coffee urn later. "You oughta come over and see Juniper. Still the best saddle horse in the county. My daughter rode her until she went off to school in Billings. She's married now. No place to keep a horse. Where's your dad?"

Lily stopped herself from asking if he would

consider selling Juniper back to her—time for that another day—and answered his question. "He's at home with his granddaughter, who's probably just about got him talked into springing for a satellite dish by now. That was her plan."

"Haven't seen him in weeks, and he sure is hogging the best hand I've ever hired." Jensen nodded at Jack. "First time you've come to one of our boring meetings, Jack."

"First time I've been to *any* of your meetings."

"Which one of you represents Mike? Or is it both?" Jensen took the top cup off the upended stack.

"You know Dad. He never wants to miss out on anything." Lily brandished her little notebook. "I took notes for him. But I really wanted to see what he's been up to since I left home. He's pretty proud of his work with the co-op."

Jack took the next two cups. "I don't know what she wrote down, but my job is to fill in all the boring parts."

"Mike's calving all done?"

"Not yet, but it's goin' good. We had a few rough days, calves dropping in the snow like road apples on some big trail ride."

"You got any free time, I could use your help." Jensen sipped the steaming black coffee and then gestured toward Jack, cup in hand. He slid a glance at Lily. "Unless you don't need the work anymore?"

"I was there when you called last week." Jack snapped the lever on the urn, and the coffee dribbled forth. "My deal with Mike hasn't changed. Beyond that, let me know what you need, and I'll work you in, just like always."

"That's what I like to hear." Jensen turned to Lily. "You tell Mike to get back in the saddle. We need him. He's got a right to be proud of what he started here."

"Well, that was awkward," Lily said, as Jack slid behind the steering wheel of his pickup.

He jammed the key into the ignition, but he forestalled turning it. Instead he gave her a curious look. "Why do you say that?"

"I don't know. I must be wearing some sort of satisfied glow."

"You mean the look of a well-serviced woman with her stud in tow?"

Her eyes widened in mock surprise. "Now, that's even more awkward."

"Not for me. I don't glow." He started the pickup and threw it into Reverse. "And I generally don't waste my time with meetings. Jensen knows that. If I'm not working cattle for Mike, I need to be working cattle for Jensen. That's what I do."

"That's not what he was getting at."

"Anything else he might be getting at doesn't

concern me." Certainly not as much as the head-lights shining in his side mirror.

"Then what was that stud remark about?"

"Indian humor." He slipped the truck into Drive and glanced her way. "What's that 'satis-fied glow' about, anyway?" He smiled. "Gotta say, it looks good on you."

"I guess we won't be going to Wolf Point any-time soon, what with all the cattle you need to be working."

"Is tomorrow soon enough? The kids have a day off from school."

"Iris doesn't."

"Different rules for different schools, I guess. Tomorrow's my day with the kids. Straight out, you wanna go with me, or would it be awkward?"

"Will I be glowing tomorrow?"

He chuckled. "Depends on where you decide to sleep tonight. You come around me, I'll be turn-ing your glow up a few notches."

"What did you learn at the meeting?"

Lily took her notebook out of her pocket and slid it across the kitchen table. Her father opened it, glanced over the first couple of pages and looked up at her. He wasn't exactly smiling, but there was real warmth in his eyes. "I knew you'd take to the idea."

"What I took were notes." She lifted one shoulder. "But who wouldn't take to the idea of producing safer beef without consigning the animal to a nasty feedlot?"

"Remember that pair of rabbits?" He stroked the open notebook as though it had a coat of soft hair. "I've thought about those rabbits a lot. The way you took care of them. They weren't pets. They were farm animals, and you knew that was the whole point of the project. But they were living, breathing creatures, and that's how you treated them. Whenever I thought about you—more and more as time went on…"

"Some of the other members want Clinton Tyree to join the co-op," she put in, thinking he would welcome a change in the subject and knowing she would. It was almost painful to imagine her father giving Hoppsie and Poppsie so much thought. "Is he still running the place? He's gotta be close to ninety."

"Mid-eighties. He'll hang on another twenty years, 'cause as soon as he goes, them worthless boys of his will sell the place and there'll be nothin' to show for—"

"Worthless *boys?* They're way older than I am."

"Old as they are, they'd never make a go of that place on their own. If they'd flown the coop same age as you did…" He sighed heavily. "It *was* a coop, wasn't it? Lily, if I could do just one day in my life over again…"

"Live and learn, Dad. Learning is key to living, right? We're not chickens. We're definitely not rabbits." The sound of her father's dry chuckle almost made her smile, but she held back. It was her turn, and she was holding the Queen of Spades. "Iris found Mom's picture box in the back of the closet in the spare room. I was surprised it was still here."

"Your mother didn't take much when she left."

"Neither did I."

"You made a clean break. I guess you both did."

"How can you make a clean break when there's blood in the mix? Your mother's eyes, your father's…" She smiled and tugged at her ample earlobe.

He pinched his even droopier one. "Sorry."

"Seriously, Dad, I tried. And I tried to hide being glad to see you when you came to Minneapolis, tried not to make too much of it, tried not to ask you for anything. I wanted to show you I didn't need you." She glanced away. "Until I did."

"Yeah, you got your best features from your mother's side. Only saw your grandmother three times, but I can sure see her in Iris. Any pictures of her in that box?"

"A few. I'm glad we have them to show Iris.

She really got into it." Lily clasped her hands together under the table and leaned forward. "But there's something else, Dad. A packet of letters addressed to Mom. They're all from the same person." He was staring at the notebook. "I'm sure it's a man."

"Did you read them?" he asked quietly without looking up.

"I was going to, but it didn't feel right, so I put them back. Did you know?"

"I didn't know there were any letters."

"But you knew there was someone else."

He looked up, allowed her to see the sadness in his eyes. "I knew she was gone long before she left."

"Did you confront her? Talk about it at all?"

"There was nothing to say." He tapped the table once with his forefinger. "Except she couldn't take you. I wasn't gonna let her, and she knew it."

"Did she try?"

He drew a deep breath and glanced past her. "Back in the cavalry days a deserter knew better than to try to take his horse. The army wouldn't waste time going after a worthless runaway, but the horse was something else."

"I was the horse?"

"You were a Reardon."

"Until I got pregnant?"

"Then you were twice the Reardon. And I

wasn't half the father you deserved. When you brought home blue ribbons and good report cards, I knew how to be your father. Build a few shelves for trophies, slip you a few extra bucks for all those A's. Even bragged you up sometimes when you weren't around to get embarrassed by it. But I was afraid to love you too much."

"Because of my mother?"

"My father was strict with us. Worked us pretty hard. Your uncle Tim took off when he was sixteen. Karen got married right out of school. I was the only one left. Didn't have much time for girls. And then women, well…I wanted a wife, sure. Had to find the right one. First time I saw your mother…" He shook his head and clicked his tongue, but he couldn't look her in the eye. "Right or wrong, I had to have her. Figured there'd be kids, boys maybe. That's how I pictured it. I never really thought about a daughter. How to talk to her, what to teach her, give her, how to be a good…"

"Parent," she said, feeling a sudden urge to cut him a break. "The one and only. It's not easy."

"She's a fine girl, your Iris. You are, too. You always have been."

"I didn't know what I was doing, Dad. I thought I did. I knew the mechanics. Insert Tab P into Slot V. I'd flirted and fooled around a little bit, and I thought all you had to do was avoid that last step, the insertion part."

Her father's face flamed.

Lily laughed. "I could never have said that to you when I was seventeen."

He stared at the notebook. "You never told me his name. My granddaughter's father."

She laughed. "I couldn't let you shoot him. Montana's a death-penalty state."

He lifted his head slowly, and the overhead light made the tiny white prickles on his chin sparkle as his mouth sketched a smile. "I just wanted to wing the son of a bitch."

"Cody. I don't consider him to be a father, though. Sperm donor at best." She considered him for a moment. "Are you curious about the letters?"

"No." He returned her level stare. "You?"

"Not now. Shall we burn them?"

"You got a mouse in your pocket, girl? I don't even wanna smell the smoke."

"I'll get rid of them before Iris gets her hands on them. To her, it's all one big soap opera."

"Reality show. She was telling me all about the shows we'll get with our new dish. Should be good entertainment if I get laid up." He slapped the table with the flat of his hand. "Yessir, I've got an appointment for next week. They're dying to try out their new radar range on me."

"You're too tough to cook, so I'm guessing CT scan."

"Stands for Cook to Tenderize, don't it?"

"Oh, Dad." Lily laid her hand over her father's and whispered, "Oh, Dad."

He nodded and laid his other hand on top of hers. His eyes glistened. A miracle. She'd never seen anything like it.

Chapter Ten

"I'd like to take a ride with Jack up to Wolf Point today," Lily told her father the next morning, when she ran into him in the living room. She was dressed and ready to go, but she hadn't had any coffee yet, and she eyed his cup. She hoped he'd left her some. "We should be back before Iris gets home from school, but if... What are you grinning about?"

"He told me." Mike glanced toward the kitchen. "Must be getting serious. I know him as well as anybody, and he's never taken *me* to Wolf Point. He says he goes up there to see his kids, but all this time I've only seen pictures." He sipped his coffee noisily and then gestured with the cup. "You can tell me if they're real."

"You doubt me, old man?" Jack challenged from the kitchen. He appeared in the doorway, cup in hand. Clearly, Lily thought, she would have to brew another pot. "I'll bring 'em down here and let them run you ragged."

"Just when I'm getting my legs back under me," Mike said.

"No pain this morning?" Lily asked her father.

"I'm back in the saddle. Right, Jack?"

Jack shifted his gaze to Lily and smiled. "I went out to the barn to make the four o'clock rounds and there he was, all saddled up."

"So you two go anywhere you want," Mike said. "Iris and me, we'll keep the home fires burning and hold down the fort."

"Just stick with the home fires." Jack nodded at Lily. "Ready when you are."

They took breakfast along on the drive to Wolf Point. Jack had already made fried-egg sandwiches and fresh coffee, so she added some fruit to the menu. They went through most of the food, and listened to and lost two radio stations before a word was said.

"You're quiet." Lily stared at the two-lane road through the windshield of Jack's big pickup. She'd offered to drive her car to save on gas, but he'd opted to keep up cowboy appearances. "What are you thinking about?"

"Good breakfast."

"You like eating on the road?"

"I do it all the time."

"When the weather's good I like to take a break at a roadside shelter and enjoy my food."

"Next time."

She nodded. "What are you really thinking about?"

"Hasn't been too long since this was the end of the oil, right about here. Remember?"

They'd just passed the sign welcoming them to the reservation, and they were still on a paved road. She didn't know why he was testing her. He knew she wouldn't remember.

If you see that sign, you've gone too far.

"I'm taking you to meet my ex-wife, and you wanna get into my head. That does sound serious." He spared her a glance. "Movin' pretty fast. Are we back to no speed limits in this state?"

"What state are you in, Jack?"

"Used to be reasonable and prudent, just like the old Montana highway law said." She detected a little smile at the corner of his mouth. "Trying to remember what that was like for me, reasonable and prudent."

What's that supposed to mean?

"I'm thinking I'm in over my head," he said quietly.

"How do you mean?" She knew, but she couldn't help herself. She had to ask.

"I'm the hired man, and you're the boss's daughter."

There had to be more to it. It was her turn to be quiet.

"I don't care what people think, you understand," he said. "Never have."

"I'm with you there." She drew a deep breath and studied the road ahead. "You think you're being...set up somehow?"

"I wouldn't allow that, no matter how far gone I was."

"In over your head," she echoed. "Far gone. What are you, a code talker?"

He laughed.

"Seriously," she said. "Just between you and me."

"As long as we stay in my trailer, it's just between you and me. There's no room for anybody else. So far, so good." Again that secret smile. "I mean, really good."

"My experience is pretty limited, but, yes, the sex is—"

"Cut it out, Lily. Don't create a misunderstanding where there isn't one." He gave her a quick glance. "I'll give it to you rock solid, all the experience you need. You can count on me there."

"In your trailer."

"Yeah. Just between us."

"We have children, Jack, and they're not just between us."

"And you have—or *will have*—a cattle ranch."

She had to puzzle over that one a bit. Finally she said, "I'm a teacher. The ranch belongs to my father."

"And I'm his hired man. If it ever came down to it, I don't know if I could be *your* hired man."

"Could you be my *man?* If it came down to it?"

He gave a dry chuckle. "I've just barely gotten to be my own man, Lily. You deserve a lot more. I'm a lot like your father. Made a lot of mistakes. I wouldn't ask you to trust a man who's just beginning to trust himself."

"Don't ask me, then. Reasonable and prudent is code for *slow down*." She pulled off a shrug quite nicely, she thought. "Which absolutely works for me. You need space? So do I."

"So much for my trailer. You don't wanna pack a dog and a cat in the same box."

"Never."

"Course not."

Edie had offered to bring the kids to his aunt's place, but since Jack had forgotten to call Auntie Sue, they were greeted at the door with quiet reserve. The old woman loved to make him squirm when he'd slighted her. She let him hug her without returning anything but a blank stare, as though the mind beneath all that gray hair had gone the way of her eyesight.

She blinked at Lily through her thick glasses. "Who's this, then?"

Jack limited his introduction to names. He knew his aunt's routine.

"You finally found a girlfriend, my boy? Or have you been keeping her a secret all this time?" She offered Lily a handshake. "You're not from around here."

"I'm from Lowdown, originally, but I moved to Minneapolis after I finished high school, and now I'm—"

"You got yourself a Lowdownian?" Auntie Sue adjusted her glasses, peered up at Jack and whispered, "How come she's got such a squeaky voice?"

Jack groaned.

She turned back to Lily. "We beat you guys every game this year."

"Auntie Sue coaches basketball from the bleachers."

"I'm the one who sounds low down," she told Lily, and then she proved her claim with a surprisingly deep, booming, "We got the spirit. Yes we do."

"Edie said she'd meet me here with the kids," Jack said. "Sorry I didn't—"

"Keep your shirt on, Jackie Mac. The woman called. They're on their way." She turned back to Lily. "What is it you do on the down low?"

"Strictly on the up-and-up, I'm an out-of-work teacher. My father's a rancher. I grew up ranching."

"And Jackie works for your father. That explains it."

Jack glanced at Lily. "Don't ask."

"There's coffee made, and fry bread. You eat fry bread?" Sue asked Lily.

"I love fry bread. Jack says yours is the best in—"

"No, he doesn't. I don't make fry bread. I have people for that." Two beats passed before the old woman laughed and tapped Lily's arm with the back of her hand. "Just kidding."

"JK, Auntie Sue. That's the latest for 'just kidding.'"

"JK," the older woman mused. "I like that." She cupped her hands around her mouth and shouted, "Wanna borrow my glasses, ref? JK."

"Don't sneak up on Auntie Sue, Wade," said a familiar voice coming in the front door. "She must be losing it."

Introducing Edie to Lily was less awkward but also less fun than introducing Auntie Sue. Edie played it straight. She'd remarried, had another kid, and she'd told Jack more than once that he ought to settle down again. But seeing him with another woman for the first time, she had little to say. She was pleasant, but she couldn't get out the door fast enough.

Becky and Wade were pretty quiet until they got to the Silverwolf, where they settled in for lunch. The occasional ding-ding-ding of a winning slot machine seemed to wind them up for a big Q and A. *Do you ride horses? What grade is your daughter in? Does she have her own cell phone? Why doesn't Dad get a cell phone?*

"Are you my dad's girlfriend?" eleven-year-old Wade wanted to know.

Lily looked at Jack. "That's a good question."

"Well, is he your boyfriend?" Becky asked. "It has to work both ways, doesn't it, Daddy?"

"That's the way I see it," Jack said. What he saw in Lily's eyes just then was an invitation, a willingness, real affection. "I want her to be my girlfriend." *Be my woman, Lily. I'm tired of being alone. Give me a chance.*

Wade turned to Lily. "You gotta say something."

"It's working both ways. I want that very much."

"You want what?" Jack asked.

"What I asked you before. Could you ever—"

"I'm your man, Lily. Any time, anywhere." He glanced at his hands on the table. Working man's hands. Hands that would fight for her, build for her, reach for her and hold her through good times and bad. "I can't promise it'll never cost you."

"I hope my credit's good."

He looked up and found her smiling. He wanted to bathe himself then and there in the warmth of her eyes.

"It's settled, then," Becky said. "Do you want to teach at our school? We've got teachers leaving all the time."

"It's never the mean ones, though," Wade said. "But you don't look mean. Do you believe in homework?"

Lily smiled. She had her glow on. "If you're interviewing me for a job, I believe in home. And I believe in work. Mostly I believe in learning, and I don't believe it has to be painful."

The house was lit up like a Christmas tree. Jack dropped Lily off at the door and drove back to his trailer. Maybe he would have a visitor tonight. Maybe not. He was all for taking it easy, but he was one dog who enjoyed spending nights in the box wrestling around with the cat.

The pounding on his door told him the cat was in his corner.

"I have to get to Glendive." It was too dark to read the piece of paper she shoved into his hand. He tried to pull her up the steps, but she grabbed his hand and tugged hard. "Dad's in the hospital. Iris is with him." She caught her breath. "I called."

"Both of them?" He reached for the jacket on the hook next to the door and jumped to the ground, forgoing the steps. "Was it an accident?"

"He fell off a horse and couldn't get up. I talked to Iris. She…she…"

"She's okay?"

"She's scared." The hand in his was cold and shaky. "She's okay. I should've called home. It's barbaric living in a dead zone."

"Nobody's dead," he muttered as he jerked the pickup door open for her.

"Dead for cell phones," she explained as he turned the key in the ignition. "Oh, God, Jack, I should have called. How fast can your pickup go?"

"Buckle up. We're goin' off-roading."

"Mom!" Iris started up from the bedside hospital chair, but she quickly settled back down again and leaned toward the head of the bed. "They're here, Grandpa."

"'Bout time." Mike's voice sounded reedy at first, but it picked up strength when Jack and Lily were within view. "Thought you were just going to Wolf Point. What'd you do, drive all the way up to Montanada?"

"Question is, what did *you* do? You gotta stay off them broncs, Mike." Jack took a quick inventory. One arm in a cast and the other hooked up to an IV bag swinging from a beeping bedside machine, facial cuts and bruises—Mike was the image of an old hard-luck cowboy.

"It was that damn dog of yours, spooked my horse." Mike turned to Iris, who was not leaving her post. "Ain't that right, girl? Iris was with me."

Iris was quiet.

"Yeah, I've really done it now." Mike tapped the cast on his arm. "Broken wing."

"Anything else?"

"Cancel that appointment. They're doing the scan here tomorrow morning." He gave a wan smile. "Might as well get it all done at once, cut down on the paperwork."

"Might as well." Jack glanced at Lily. In the garish light she looked pale.

"How'd it go up there in Wolf Point?" Mike asked his daughter. "Anybody claim to be related to this guy?"

"Two lovely children, for starters," she said

quietly. "Becky's Iris's age, and Wade looks just like his father."

Mike smiled, then said, "We were headed out to check cows when I got throwed. Last I saw, we had a couple of heavies, and we've only got eight still holdin' out." He lifted the arm with the needle taped to it. "You take these girls home now. That's where you're needed."

"I'm staying," Lily said.

"You're going home." He sounded firm for the moment, but he was fading. "Please," he said to Jack. "I don't like it here. Won't be long before my sweet disposition goes south, and I don't wanna lose any ground we might've gained." He glanced at Lily. "We have, haven't we?"

"We have." She sat down on the edge of the bed, clearly afraid to touch him, afraid not to. Afraid to be turned away. "Let me stay."

"I have a feelin' you'll have plenty of chances to hang around the hospital in the next few weeks if that's the way you wanna spend your time. Right now I want you all to go home and let the nurses have their way with me." Mike feebly patted the mattress, and Lily laid her hand over his. "*Home.* It's always been yours, Lily." He turned to Jack. "Yours, too, if you want it."

"First you give out orders, then you sound like some old drunk trying to give everything away."

Keep it light, Jack told himself as he nodded toward the IV stand. "What's in that bag?"

"I don't know, but it's better than a bottle."

Jack smiled. "How soon before you pass out?"

"Soon as you stop hoverin' over me."

"I'm coming back tomorrow," Lily said.

"I've got plans for tomorrow. Call first." Mike closed his eyes, satisfied with having the final word. "All booked up. Hooked up. Get cooked up tomorrow." He coughed, quieted and muttered, "Radar range."

"I'll see to the chores and be back tomorrow." Lily leaned down and kissed her father's forehead.

Mike's eyes were closed, but he smiled.

Two healthy calves had hit the ground while they were gone, and Jack counted three more cows in the early stages with no signs of distress. With any luck calving would be over in a day or two, but if he had any luck coming, he didn't want to use it up on the cows.

He put up his horse and headed for his trailer, but on the way he noticed a fire outside the machine shed. It was contained in the burning barrel, flames writhing like dancers, embers flashing and floating into the night.

He joined Lily, held his hands out for warmth, pressed his side against hers. "Can't sleep?"

"I had to take the trash out." She was mesmerized by the fire. "Those letters I told you about. I wanted them out of the house."

"Did you read them?"

"No. Well, I started to. They were from a man, just as we thought. *I* thought. But I'm burning the details. He doesn't matter, whoever he is. He's nothing to me." She shrugged. He liked the way it felt against his arm. "I told Dad about the guy. He already had it figured out."

"He didn't want to read them, either?"

"No. But for me, it kind of helps in a way, knowing why. Nothing to do with me." She looked up at him. He loved the firelight in her eyes. "Kicking me out probably didn't have much to do with me, either."

"Hurt people *hurt* people. They tell you stuff like that when you're trying to get sober. You turn a deaf ear at first, and then you let it sink in, and then have yourself a good cry. What doesn't send you running back to the bottle makes you stronger."

"Cowboys cry?"

"Don't tell anybody."

"It'll be our secret. The first of many we'll share if you…" She slid her arm around his back. "…meant what you said at lunch."

He turned her toward him. "I meant every

word. I'm in love with you, Lily. I never thought I'd feel this way again, but I do, and it feels good."

"I've *never* felt this way before." She laid her hand on his cheek, which was cold to the touch but dear to her. "I love you, Jack."

He smiled gently. "How can you be sure?"

"How can I not? It fills me up. I feel like I'm—"

He covered her mouth with a kiss that consumed them both, stealing breath and giving it back, then stealing it again until he knew her conviction as surely as he knew his own. He pulled her tight against him and simply held her.

She tucked her face into the opening of his jacket, and he felt the warmth of the fire on her cheek and the chill of the night on the tip of her nose.

"I'm afraid of what they'll find in those X-rays," she whispered. "All this time we could've been closer. Why did we waste it?"

"I ask myself that all the time." He kissed the top of her head. "Maybe it had to be that way so you could be where you are now."

"With you?"

"With all of us. Whatever happens now, none of us is alone."

"And I thought cowboys were all hat and no cattle."

"No way. I've got a horse, and even a trailer to

keep him in." He chuckled. "And a pretty good nest egg since I stopped blowing my wages."

"So what are we going to do, Jack? I'm still the boss's daughter."

"Marry me and I'll be your man. Your ever-lovin' man." He leaned back so he could see the firelight in her eyes. "Otherwise I'll be riding off into the sunset."

"I'll be your wife, Jackie Mac." She cuddled him close and whispered, "I'll be your ever-lovin' woman."

* * * * *

COMING NEXT MONTH
from Harlequin® Special Edition®
AVAILABLE MARCH 19, 2013

#2251 HER HIGHNESS AND THE BODYGUARD
The Bravo Royales
Christine Rimmer
Princess Rhiannon Bravo-Calabretti has loved only one man in her life—orphan turned soldier Captain Marcus Desmarais—but he walked away knowing that she deserved more than a commoner. Years later, fate stranded them together overnight in a freak spring blizzard...and gave them an unexpected gift!

#2252 TEN YEARS LATER...
Matchmaking Mamas
Marie Ferrarella
Living in Tokyo, teaching English, Sebastian Hunter flees home to his suddenly sick mother's side just in time to attend his high school reunion. Brianna MacKenzie, his first love, looks even better than she had a decade ago...but can he win her over for the second and final time?

#2253 MARRY ME, MENDOZA
The Fortunes of Texas: Southern Invasion
Judy Duarte
Because of a stipulation in her employment contract, Nicole Castleton needs to marry before she can become the CEO of Castleton Boots. Her plan to reunite with ex-high school sweetheart Miguel Mendoza was strictly business—until their hearts got in the way!

#2254 A BABY IN THE BARGAIN
The Camdens of Colorado
Victoria Pade
After what her great-grandfather did to his family, bitter Gideon Thatcher refuses to hear a word of January Camden's apology...or get close to the beautiful brunette. Plus, she's desperate to have a baby, and Gideon does *not* see children in his future. But after spending time together, they may find they share more than just common ground....

#2255 THE DOCTOR AND MR. RIGHT
Rx for Love
Cindy Kirk
Dr. Michelle Kerns has a "no kids" rule when it comes to dating men...until she meets her hunky neighbor who has a child—a thirteen-year-old girl to be exact! Her mind says no, but maybe this one rule *is* meant to be broken!

#2256 THE TEXAN'S FUTURE BRIDE
Byrds of a Feather
Sheri WhiteFeather
Suffering from amnesia, J.D. wandered aimlessly through Buckshot Hills until Jenna Byrd offered the injured cowboy a place to stay. Slowly memories flood back to him, but what he remembers makes him want to run away from love—*fast.* Yet why can't he keep himself out of beautiful Jenna's embrace?

You can find more information on upcoming Harlequin® titles,
free excerpts and more at www.HarlequinInsideRomance.com.

HSECNM0313

REQUEST YOUR FREE BOOKS!

2 FREE NOVELS PLUS 2 FREE GIFTS!

♦ HARLEQUIN®

SPECIAL EDITION

Life, Love & Family

YES! Please send me 2 FREE Harlequin® Special Edition novels and my 2 FREE gifts (gifts are worth about $10). After receiving them, if I don't wish to receive any more books, I can return the shipping statement marked "cancel." If I don't cancel, I will receive 6 brand-new novels every month and be billed just $4.49 per book in the U.S. or $5.24 per book in Canada. That's a savings of at least 14% off the cover price! It's quite a bargain! Shipping and handling is just 50¢ per book in the U.S. and 75¢ per book in Canada.* I understand that accepting the 2 free books and gifts places me under no obligation to buy anything. I can always return a shipment and cancel at any time. Even if I never buy another book, the two free books and gifts are mine to keep forever.

235/335 HDN FVTV

Name	(PLEASE PRINT)

Address		Apt. #

City	State/Prov.	Zip/Postal Code

Signature (if under 18, a parent or guardian must sign)

Mail to the Harlequin® Reader Service:
IN U.S.A.: P.O. Box 1867, Buffalo, NY 14240-1867
IN CANADA: P.O. Box 609, Fort Erie, Ontario L2A 5X3

Want to try two free books from another line?
Call 1-800-873-8635 or visit www.ReaderService.com.

* Terms and prices subject to change without notice. Prices do not include applicable taxes. Sales tax applicable in N.Y. Canadian residents will be charged applicable taxes. Offer not valid in Quebec. This offer is limited to one order per household. Not valid for current subscribers to Harlequin Special Edition books. All orders subject to credit approval. Credit or debit balances in a customer's account(s) may be offset by any other outstanding balance owed by or to the customer. Please allow 4 to 6 weeks for delivery. Offer available while quantities last.

Your Privacy—The Harlequin® Reader Service is committed to protecting your privacy. Our Privacy Policy is available online at www.ReaderService.com or upon request from the Harlequin Reader Service.

We make a portion of our mailing list available to reputable third parties that offer products we believe may interest you. If you prefer that we not exchange your name with third parties, or if you wish to clarify or modify your communication preferences, please visit us at www.ReaderService.com/consumerschoice or write to us at Harlequin Reader Service Preference Service, P.O. Box 9062, Buffalo, NY 14269. Include your complete name and address.

***

How could this have happened?

Rhiannon Bravo-Calabretti, Princess of Montedoro, could not believe it. Honestly. What were the odds?

One in ten, maybe? One in twenty? She supposed that it could have been just the luck of the draw. After all, her country was a small one and there were only so many rigorously trained bodyguards to be assigned to the members of the princely family.

However, when you added in the fact that Marcus Desmarais wanted nothing to do with her ever again, reasonable odds became pretty much no-way-no-how. Because he would have said no.

So why hadn't he?

A moment later she realized she knew why: because if he refused the assignment, his superiors might ask questions. Suspicion and curiosity could be roused, and he wouldn't have wanted that.

Stop.

Enough. Done. She was simply not going to think about it—about *him*—anymore.

She needed to focus on the spare beauty of this beautiful wedding in the small town of Elk Creek, Montana. Her sister was getting married. Everyone was seated in the little church.

Still, *he* would be standing. In back somewhere by the doors, silent and unobtrusive. Just like the other security people. Her shoulders ached from the tension, from the certainty he was watching her, those eerily level, oh-so-serious, almost-green eyes staring twin holes in the back of her head.

It doesn't matter. Forget about it, about him.

It didn't matter why he'd been assigned to her. He was there to protect her, period. And it was for only this one day and the evening. Tomorrow she would fly home again. And be free of him. Forever.

She could bear anything for a single day. It had been a shock, that was all. And now she was past it.

She would simply ignore him. How hard could that be?

***

Don't miss HER HIGHNESS AND THE BODYGUARD, coming in April 2013 in Harlequin® Special Edition®.

And look for Alice's story,
HOW TO MARRY A PRINCESS, only from
Harlequin® Special Edition®, in November 2013.

SPECIAL EDITION

Life, Love and Family

There's magic—and love—in those Texas hills!

THE TEXAN'S FUTURE BRIDE
by Sheri WhiteFeather

Suffering from amnesia, J.D. wandered aimlessly through Buckshot Hills until Jenna Byrd offered the injured cowboy a place to stay. Slowly memories seep back to him, but what he remembers makes him want to run away from love—*fast*. Yet why can't he keep himself out of beautiful Jenna's embrace?

Look for the second title in the *Byrds of a Feather* miniseries next month!

Available in April 2013 from Harlequin Special Edition wherever books are sold.